Chronicles Of The Jungle Mom

To order additional copies, please contact us.
BookSurge, LLC
www.booksurge.com
1-866-308-6235
orders@booksurge.com

Chronicles Of The Jungle Mom

Michele Kohan

Publisher
2003

Chronicles of the Jungle Mom

————————————————————————

Table of Contents

I dedicate this book to my children and to the
children of Puerto Viejo, who were my inspiration.

Preface

The Chronicles of the Jungle Mom is a compilation of newsletters that were sent via email to family and friends back in the United States during our stay in Costa Rica. With the exception of changing the names of some of the individuals mentioned, the text remains largely unedited from the original version.

The original intent of the Chronicles was to provide a weekly update of our new 'adventures'. However, as events unfolded, the writing of the Chronicles became almost a daily exercise. I wrote about the events of the day by the light of a candle each night and sent them via email from the local Internet café the next morning. As time went on, my inbox began to fill with feedback from people all over the United States. The Chronicles soon took on a life of their own, serving not only as a reminder for years to come of the adventures we had that summer in Costa Rica, but also as an adhesive of sorts, strengthening and renewing bonds with the family and friends I had left behind.

There were many reasons for the move to Costa Rica, but primarily the idea was born of a desire to become involved with El Puente, a grassroots non-profit organization run by Barry and Nanci Stevens. This couple has chosen to dedicate their incredible energy toward improving the quality of life for the local indigenous BriBri of Puerto Viejo. The Steven's home serves as the 'Bridge' fostering the needs of the people who make the daily trek from their dwelling place deep within the Rainforest. The services provided include a soup kitchen three days per week, small business loans, and financial assistance enabling families to enroll their children in the local public school.

El Puente is indeed a 'Bridge' in every sense of the word, and operation of the Bridge takes place 24 hours a day, seven days a week. Each and every day holds both challenges and rewards. The needs of the indigenous always take precedence over the Steven's own needs or comfort. It is hard to put into words the gratitude I feel toward Barry and Nanci, but will only say that the life lessons I learned in just ten short weeks largely outweigh much of what has been learned over an entire lifetime. Although we have relocated back to the States for the time being, my heart remains in Puerto Viejo; and the faces of the indigenous people are forever burned in my memories.

Twenty-five percent of the proceeds from the sale of this book will be donated to the continued operation of El Puente. To find out more about the Steven's work and to keep abreast of the latest updates, access their web site at www.elpuente-thebridge.org.

Barry and Nanci Stevens—Founders of El Puente

Chapter 1.
The Arrival

June 7th through June 12th

It's hard to start at the beginning, as the last few days have been so full of events and emotions. Putting down thoughts as they came to mind seemed the only way to keep track, with time perhaps later to expand on each story. Here's a little to get you started, with more to come each week...

The departure...well, the phrase speaks for itself, but that having been said, the kids were awesome. The day started with an emotional goodbye with family, and ended with an emotional arrival for all of us.

Silence in the back seat was a welcome respite from the usual brawling. I had wondered why my brother-in-law had put the children four seats behind us in his eleven-passenger van, but I guess having six kids has taught him a thing or two. The most we heard was a distant word here and there filtered through the massive piles of trunks that were packed from floor to ceiling. Arrival at the airport came more quickly than anticipated, and even the task of getting the twelve trunks checked went off smoothly. Ok, we raised a few eyebrows, and maybe even the sympathy of the attendant, who said the best she could do was charge us for four, rather than six extra bags. But gratitude toward my brother-in-law could not be hidden as he helped unload those trunks and arranged for a porter to wheel them all in for us.

Past the check-in, now on to security. Amazingly, nobody was concerned about the injectible epinephrine I was begging to carry on the plane for my youngest child—they didn't even want to see the letter that had been so meticulously prepared on our pediatrician's letterhead. Another bridge crossed, and two hours to wait—two hours to wait *with children.* This was the thing I had dreaded the most, but thanks to the novelty of airport bathrooms and water fountains—and I admit, a laptop computer with games—we made it through the two hours.

The flight…well, let's just say—I'm not fond of flying, and Alex is terrified of flying. *Did I mention we all get sick flying?* We took off with lips quivering and little hands clutching the pendant of St. Christopher given to me by my sister the day before—a guardian to keep us safe. But once again—there's something to be said about bathrooms, free soda, and those little packets of sugar, creamer, and itty-bitty spoons that kept the kids entertained for the entire three hours—no kidding.

The arrival…never let the smile-less faces fool you. We breezed through immigration as the man-without-a-smile haphazardly checked off every line on our forms and methodically stamped all three passports. There were no questions as to the kids having different last names, no questions as to "Where is their father?" and no request for the notarized statements that I had so painstakingly drawn up. *Todo esta bien.*

Finding our trunks…ten minutes waiting by the rolling luggage belt yielded nothing, and then a sign that said something in Spanish about 'Oversized Baggage—Belt # 4' caught my eye as all three of us simultaneously spotted the trunks piled in a corner across the baggage claim area. Go figure—near 'Belt # 4'. Arguably, our trunks were not really oversized, coming in a full inch below the allowed sixty-two linear inches, but I suppose the fact that using hard plastic trunks in lieu of the average suitcase somehow put them in a category of their own. They do stand out in a crowd.

Getting the group of backpackers who were engrossed in a deep conversation that involving mapping out their entire itinerary (how dare I butt in!) to get their paperwork and elbows off of MY trunks was yet another story...

The kids and I started loading the luggage onto three of the—hmmm—*shopping carts*—that were provided, but before we had even gotten the first trunk lifted above the ground, nice-looking-man-in-the-red-shirt appeared out of nowhere and said 'I can get you a *'bigger cart'*. In the snap of a finger, there he was with the Big Cart—much more accommodating, and better yet, he single-handedly loaded all the trunks onto the cart for us. Ok, they were precariously perched, not methodically stacked as they had been in the departure airport, but for goodness sake—this IS a third-world country! We had a hard time keeping up with him as he made his way toward the customs checkpoint. Small talk with the red-shirt guy—What? Are you moving to Costa Rica? Yes, yes we are... Big smile—Esta bien!

Then the encounter with no-smile Customs Guy. *I guess it's part of their job description.* Customs Guy is the one in charge of the only machine that you must pass every piece of luggage you brought through—before you are allowed to walk out of the airport. Normally you *and only you* are responsible for this dubious task, with no-smile customs guy watching as you struggle to shove each suitcase upward onto the little rollies that don't actually roll. Thank the Lord once again for red-shirt guy. He unloaded and put through every trunk for us. As he did that, I simultaneously kept my eyes on both children— who by the way were moving in different directions—while skirting questions in Spanish from Customs Guy as to why we were carrying twelve trunks into the country with us. Several times the question—And how long are you staying? But he kept getting the standard answer—Three months, just three months…*Of course* we won't be overstaying our 90-day tourist Visa! Yes, yes, I'll be 'volunteering' for a soup kitchen—yes, some of the clothing and toys are for the BriBri children—all of this stuff *couldn't possibly* belong to *my* two children!

Whew, another bridge crossed, then we met our drivers, who by the way, offered to score us any kind of *electrodomesticas* we might need later on down the road…since we obviously weren't bringing the family TV with us…must be a side business of some sort.

The trip down the mountain…Four hours in a van with tired, cranky children. The only thing that kept me sane was keeping my eye on the windshield, which didn't seem to be defrosting, as we traversed down the treacherous mountain roads in the pouring rain. "In weather like this, we must watch out for landslides," the driver commented.

The drivers here have a different way of doing things. The goal is—get there as fast as you can. It's a race—it's always a race. The guy who passes the most semi-trucks on the windy mountain road, in the rain, with no defrosters, and gets there first—es el *Ganador!* The Winner! *We won because we got there alive.*

The arrival. Ok, the second arrival…at the casita. Pulled up, backed in, and the first thing the landlord said was—We didn't realize you were bringing *so much luggage*! One look at the house—did I mention the word 'casita' not 'casa'. The suffix 'ita' if you are unaware—refers to small, pequeno, not Large in any way, shape or form…One look at the house and we realized we had more luggage than house. The trunks were haphazardly stacked on our outdoor living room floor and the driver and landlords quickly disappeared.

Culture shock and overtired, cranky kids do not mix… is there any need to say more? As the landlord's wife was walking away, she mentioned that it wouldn't be wise to leave anything of value in the 'outdoor' room. After the three of us overtired cranky kids managed to get all twelve trunks off the outdoor living room floor and into the kitchen and upstairs bedrooms—we went to bed. It was about 10:00 by then, midnight by the standards we were used to. But mañana is another day...

Chapter 2.
The First Days—Culture Shock

The great thing about Costa Rica is that your body self-adjusts to the environment. You wake up at 4 am sharp every day when the birds start making every noise imaginable and you're dead-tired by 6:30 pm just after sunset...no more living behind concrete walls. The other funny thing about waking up at 4 am is that when it's only 7:15 am it feels like it should be much later. We found that out the morning after we arrived—when we rang the bell on my future employer's gate and watched him exit his bedroom in his bathrobe...Thank goodness they are forgiving people. We were invited in for coffee, then eventually breakfast and a long trip to Limon for Big Groceries, which cannot be had in Puerto Viejo. Many profuse apologies, and we made a concerted effort to stay away for the next day or two out of respect for 'The Error'.

Limon is Hot...and it is always ten degrees hotter in the car. The second stop after grocery shopping was the eyeglass repair shop where Nanci had dropped off her glasses for minor repairs. Unfortunately, the eyeglass repairman had to go out to find more screws. What would seem the obvious in the US is not always the case here.

The highlight of our morning was watching an elderly peddler push his cart up the street, stopping every so often to hack open a coconut with his machete. These coconuts are called pipas, kept in a cooler on ice, and served with a straw. Although my kids had been fascinated with the concept at first, their first 40-minute ride to Limon in an non-air conditioned car, including two transit stops, and the eventual wait for the glasses had taken its toll—they didn't have the energy to even ask for a cold coconut!

Did you know Transitos carry Uzi's? Something brought in and purchased from the Russians years ago I've been told—*and they don't smile.* But that could have something to do with standing in the 90-degree baking sun in flak suits holding their Uzi's in the ready-to-shoot position. *We* actually felt sorry for them...

Side Trip...a la derecha... On the way home from Limon, we took a side trip into BriBri so Nanci could place her order for this weekend's food bolsas. She's found a great store there that will bag the items for her, tie the bundles, and have them ready for pickup on Friday afternoon. The only items that need to be added are a carton of eggs and a package of galletas—salted crackers, which are placed carefully in the top of each bag on Saturday morning just before distribution.

The process of compiling the bulging bolsas of food staples used to take much longer, and entailed driving all over town to find the necessary items, and then bagging them all by hand. With the continued increase in the number of bolsas distributed each week, hand bagging had become a dubious task.

The bolsa order is usually handled over the phone, but Nanci made the trip for our benefit, and thus our introduction to the sleepy mountain town of BriBri. Nestled between the Talamanca mountain range, the town itself consists of one main street and three or four side streets lined with small businesses and local hardwood houses. Howler monkeys can be heard at almost any time of day, and a mist continually rises from the fringes of town, giving it a feeling of tranquility and an odd mystical aura.

We had the good fortune of purchasing a large bunch of bananas from a local indigenous woman along the way. For the equivalent of about $1.25 we received about $15 worth of what bananas would cost in a grocery store in the States. I hope Nanci was right when she said they will ripen one row at a time...and we're banking on the fact that it will be soon, before my daughter (whose current diet consists of cheese sandwiches and bananas) begins to fade away. My little girl has been watching those bananas like a hawk for the past three days...

Barry came driving up soon after we arrived home from the trip to Limon; the car in fact, was still warm. *There's a sloth in our yard and the kids must see it!* An incredible opportunity, and one that simple could not be refused. So we put lunch aside and jumped back into the car. The sloth or *perezoso* was not only in the yard, he was methodically making his way up the bars on the Steven's bedroom window—an exact replica of the sculpture Nanci had artistically crafted and placed on their front entranceway. Amazing creature, so docile, looking back and forth, blinking both eyes at once—he had us mesmerized. We even reached through the screen to pet his nose when he extended his head toward us out of curiosity. Kind of reminded us of E.T., the Extraterrestrial. He finally made his way down the bars via a 2 x 2 piece of wood that was leaning against the house. Nanci struggled to unlatch him from the metal box on the ground that he grabbed onto next, and managed to pick him up and point him in the other direction—toward the Rainforest and away from the highway.

Later that afternoon, we finally made it down to the heavenly black sand beach—Playa Negra. Here the water is warm, and the best time to go is after 4:30 when the sun starts to go down. *Perfect.* I lay in the water for at least an hour just letting the waves carry me in, swimming back and forth, and watching the kids catch sand dollars. Did you know sand dollars are actually live creatures, living in the shallow waters, just beneath the sand? They're brown in color with thousands of little legs wiggling underneath, a far cry from the dried white sand dollars we'd seen for sale in the Florida tourist areas. In two days time, we've managed to pick up at least fifty of them, easily grasped between our toes.

Crabs Galore... My young son's favorite book, entitled *'Commotion in the Ocean'* was the first thing that came to mind as I watched the crabs scurry sideways across the hot black sand. There is a wide variation in the crab species, ranging from little white ones measuring a few inches across, to huge crabs the size of two fists with sun-hardened red or blue shells. Douglas found his pastime in a little patch of wet ground just outside our residence gate where hundreds of crabs continually peek in and out of their holes. He managed to catch a little one, was soon pinched by a medium size one, and I am sure that by the end of the week he'll have a meal-size crab for me...then I'll just have to figure out how to cook it.

Chapter 3.
Settling In—The Wonders of Our New Life

Living with bug dust and ants... There are two things about living in a house with no walls—bug dust and ants. And there are lots of both. I found out quite by accident that when you sweep the upstairs sleeping rooms, the downstairs rooms are suddenly covered with little sprinkles of what I'll kindly to as 'bug dust' and black sand granules—go figure? It may have something to do with the space between the floorboards. It took me two days to figure out why the refrigerator top was dirty every morning.

And the ants, ah those wonderful wild *crazy ants.* Everywhere. We see them inside, outside, on the counters, on the walls. Thank goodness they don't bite. We're used to them now. The crazy ants are a part of our family.

Colocha explained to me there are several different species of ants. First, there are the crazy ants—wild, running in every direction. There is no way to get rid of them, so we must *commune* with them. Secondly, there are the itty-bitty bite ants. I was introduced to this species one afternoon as my arm, draped over the side railing of the living room, suddenly felt as if a pan of boiling oil had been poured over it. These are akin to Florida fire ants. Then there are the larger fire ants that build the nests along the beach road extending six to eight feet across. A small child could fall down into the center of one. I'm told this species bites too, but we haven't dared to get close enough to one of the nests to find out.

Lastly, I received a tutorial about the Army Ants. These guys apparently come in to 'clean house' a few times a year. When the Army Ants come, you leave. No ifs, ands, or buts. When you return, they are gone and your house has been cleaned of all debris. They march in columns eight inches wide and you can see them coming across the yard. Just get out of the way, I'm told...

Bats in the belfries... We have a fruit bat that insists on coming in under the eaves and then frantically trying to get out of the kid's bedroom...The kids were all excited the first time it happened...Mommy, there's a bird in our room, oh, it's soooo cute! Poor thing, it got in and now it can't get out. No, that's not a bird sweeties, it's a flying mammal...*screams and hysteria...*

I talked to Colocha about the bat and was pretty much told it's just something you live with here. No, they don't bite; they are just annoying—Why? Because they leave bat dung in the house...thus the plug in bat-repellant that was emitting a low pitched sound in the bathroom downstairs. When I inquired about this contraption, Colocha was quick to say she used it to rotate through the various houses that she owns—*it does not belong to this house alone*—and she promptly took the bat repellant with her. Colocha also said the little fruit bats are not really a problem, just a nuisance. However, the larger bat that will come in and hang from your wall or clothes line, *that one is a problem*—Why? Bigger, more disgusting dung, of course!

Colocha and Mauricio are our landlords. Mauricio is a local indigenous BriBri man and Colocha is European, I believe, although I can't quite figure out her accent as she adjusts it so well to the particular language she is speaking.

They've been married for 23 years. Colocha said that when she married Mauricio, they lived more in the indigenous way. Cooking over an open fire, living in an indigenous home, which consists of simply a platform and a tin roof. There has only been electricity and municipal 'potable' water in Puerto Viejo for about ten years or so now. Things have changed a lot. Colocha said people come into her house now and comment on how 'simply' she lives—yet she feels they live in luxury. Their home sports a television, every morning I hear an electric blender as fresh fruit juice is prepared for breakfast, and a real washing machine occupies the bottom floor of the dwelling. It seems with a bit of sadness that Colocha describes the old way of living and the technology that has slowly crept into their lives.

Colocha explained to me that only a few pieces of clothing are necessary, and clothing wears out quickly due to the tropical environment. Once worn for even a few moments, a piece of clothing must be washed; otherwise it will start to show black spots from a particular strain of mold that begins to grow on the fabric. I realized immediately that the contents of five of the six trunks of clothing we brought with us are utterly useless now and can't even really be donated because none of it is practical. The denim shorts and cotton t-shirts are ok for the time being, but will soon be replaced with more typical Caribbean garb. Alex took off a polo shirt this afternoon and replaced it with a lighter weight scoop neck t-shirt because *the collar is too hot mommy...*

We've learned a few things in our first week here. To accept things as they are, to cohabitate and commune with the nature that surrounds us. To live the Caribbean way is to live with nature, or more appropriately said, to live along side of it, and to have respect for it.

Everything is a learning process. Take the garbage, for example. All food scraps must be immediately swept out and tables wiped down, dishes washed. Food scraps are put into a Tupperware container with a lid that is marked *basura organica* and is then throw over the fence to the chickens each morning. Plastic water and soda bottles are recycled, as are soda cans. The remaining garbage, such as yogurt containers and cracker wrappers, must be rinsed out before putting it in the trash can underneath the sink—or, you guessed it, the number of ants triples almost instantly. The mesh garbage 'holding containers' located out front near the gate are meant to keep the horses out until Tuesday pickup. I admit the garbage downtown gets a bit smelly by the time the weekend rolls around.

Where is the handle? The first day, we ran into a few problems with the keys to the house. There is a trick to using these keys, a certain way to twist the key to the right and yank the door-with-no-handle forward all at the same time. I think we finally got the hang of it, but not without calling the landlady over—twice—until she took the time to give us a demonstration.

Zap! The 'suicide shower' is an interesting concept in technology. A contraption much like an enlarged showerhead, this compact water heater hangs from the overhead shower faucet, with raw wires running in every direction, which eventually lead to the electrical outlet. When functioning properly, it heats the water as it runs through the faucet. The main thing to remember when using the hot water setting in the suicide shower is *Never Touch the Metal Handle with a Wet Hand.*

After a few feeble attempts at using the suicide shower, I called the landlords over. Mauricio found no fault with the ground wire, so he wrapped a piece of plastic with duct tape over the handle to prevent another 'zap' from occurring. A dry washcloth has become a permanent fixture in the shower though, because somehow, I still cannot bring myself to touch the shower handle with my bare hand.

Alex and Starry...wish I had a picture of this one, but unfortunately, our desire to save this magnificent creature overcame the urge to run back to the house for the camera.

All I heard was a loud screech from the beach and found Alex looking down—horrified at the gigantic starfish that lay at her feet.

The animal was approximately the size of, well, I'd say about the size of the laptop I'm working on...and it was definitely alive. Millions of little tiny feet wiggled underneath. The top surface was rough to the touch. What a wonderful, beautiful creature; I've never seen anything so amazing. Douglas loved it and of course wanted to make it a pet but Alex and I convinced him to let it go. He threw it back into the water in hopes it will find it's way back to where it came from. We haven't seen Starry again but he'll live on always in our memories of these first exciting days.

Chapter 4.
Introduction to Soup Kitchen Day.

June 11th

Well, to skip a few beats and move onto today...Our first experience at the soup kitchen as a family. We decided to forego the long walk into Puerto to check out the Saturday morning farmer's market and instead saved our energy for helping Barry and Nanci at El Puente. The kids are settling down nicely now and I decided to give the experience a try.

It was an exhausting day, but very rewarding. There were plenty of 'helpers' at El Puente today. Joyce, the Juice Queen. A retired lady who lives down the way, Joyce comes to make the juice—solely to make the juice. Sue, an Americana writer who has become a fixture every Saturday at El Puente, helping to wash and dry the piles of dirty dishes. Then there were the two young Scottish girls—I couldn't pronounce their names if I tried. Both beautiful, white-blond girls with lovely accents, they are in their third month of a six-month internship stay with the indigenous BriBri. These girls actually live on the 'interior' of the reservation, in a typical indigenous dwelling, complete with snakes and scorpions. They arrived at El Puente with backpacks in tow. Finally, there was the sweet college student from Minnesota, living here for several months while she completes a thesis on Ecotourism.

The day started at 9 am as we arrived at the Steven's place. Time passes slowly for the first hour or so, then the pace picks up and one must keep focused in order to contend with it all. It wasn't a typical day with all the extra hands but I'm told there are many Saturdays that Barry, Nanci, Joyce and Sue have gone it alone. I wasn't sure how this would all turn out but I must say—my kids were troopers. They learned quite a few Spanish phrases, made some friends, and actually drew a few smiles from the BriBri people as they served throughout the day. *Quiere café? Quiere jugo? Mas leche? Mas sopa? Ya termino?* Or simply *Ya?* We've found already that much of the Spanish previously studied is abbreviated here. I've noticed many colloquialisms, such as 'Bueno' the shortened form of Buenos Dias, which will eventually need to be learned and added to our growing vocabulary.

Friends and family gather at El Puente on a typical busy Saturday

The day ended at about 3 pm when we finally started the long, hot walk back toward the house. The kids talked me into a second stop at Jeffrey's, the local corner store, owned by—you guessed it—Jeffrey, a Rastafarian and the Steven's landlord—for another ice cream. *We recognized Jeffrey as the man who helped Alex untangle her leg from the pedal of her bicycle yesterday.*

A second ice cream is not usually on the agenda, but I'd say the kids deserved it just this once. Alex refilled at least six full pitchers of hand-squeezed juice into glass after glass, and Douglas delivered many a cup of café and even helped clear up the dirty dishes. We became wrapped up in the midst of it all, and I believe the children felt the great need that is here, managing somehow to overcome their own exhaustion in order to help keep the day running smoothly.

After soup kitchen, we took a nice dip in the ocean with Nanci, Sue, and three of Maria's children—Alejandro, Maria, and William. Douglas and Alejandro seem to have hit it off. Douglas was persistent throughout much of the day, and repeatedly asked Alejandro "Quiere buscar animals?" a phrase that roughly translates to "Do you want to look for animals?"

Alex and Maria have made many woeful looks and shy smiles toward each other, but nothing concrete has developed yet. These things take time; and the BriBri kids are notoriously shy. The children tend to keep to themselves even in the public school they attend. Barry and Nanci noted that for many months they would interact with the kids one day at the house, and the very next day the children would act as if they had never met before, so the process had to begin all over again.

Nanci asked my kids today how they like it here in Costa Rica. Their answer was a resounding "Great!" followed by a dialogue of all the new and wonderful things they've seen, learned about, and the friends they've made. No matter what the months ahead bring, I'll never regret the decision I've made to move here. I'm not sure where fate will take us next, but I know for certain we'll never regret our time spent in Paradise.

Chapter 5.
Rough Roads

June 13th

Today was a hard day. But we knew there would be a few of those. I believe it was Mike Murdock, the television evangelist, who made the statement "How you react in the face of adversity determines how God will reward you in the future," or something to that effect. I had to remind myself today that God was watching. We decided early this morning to take a bicycle ride down the road that runs in front of the beach and opted to explore in the opposite direction this time. We didn't get far before Douglas had one of his 'crashes'. Not your average bicycle wobble and falling over crash. No, Douglas does it in a Big Way—and several times a day. He's started wearing the tall rubber snake boots to protect at least the bottom of his legs from the gravel roads.

Our next venture was to go into Puerto on two missions—the first, being a hunt for the Farmacia to find some sort of crème to put on the rash that now consumes Douglas' entire trunk area. It started with a brush against some foliage in North Carolina two weeks ago and has evolved into a fine rash pretty much all over his body. The fact that the rash doesn't really itch has me puzzled, as we first thought it might have been poison oak. It's unsightly, but not really bothersome. In any event, the bicycle that seems to be the least sturdy, *having already lost a pedal,* managed this morning to break it's chain, necessitating an unexpected change of plans. A trip to the Ferreteria for repairs was in order; and once again, we received excellent customer service. The salesman repeated the now-familiar phrase—"Estamos aqui para servirle." *We're here to serve you.* The chain made it into Puerto then fell off again on the way home.

The Jungle Café was still closed at 8:30 am, although the sign said opens at 8:00 am. Another of those little things one must become accustomed to. We soon found the Farmacia, followed by a stop at a roadside stand for a pipa. The kids had a shaved ice with extremely sugary syrup. As Douglas watched the elderly vendor shave the ice off the block by hand, he asked "This is the old fashioned way, right?" Yes, Douglas, everything here is done the old fashioned way. After the shaved ices were eaten, the words spoken by the nurse at the local health department prior to our departure echoed through our minds. *Never eat ice with your drinks...*I wonder if eating a little ice with your syrup falls into the same category?

Por fin! The Jungle Café was now open and we entered as the second customers in the place. I'm told it fills up quickly, so this was indeed a blessing. We set up our account and managed to quickly answer two emails and zip out the newsletter. Only 29 minutes of the hour paid for used up. Not bad.

A stop at Buen Precio, the best grocery store in town. Ok, the only grocery store in town, except for Jeffrey's and that doesn't really count. Jeffrey's is more like a pared down Kwik King, full of the staples needed to carry you through until a trip into town can be arranged. Our shopping trip yielded an oversized water bottle that filled the entire bicycle basket, some boiled ham, the only commodity that Douglas will eat and typically hard to come by, a package of bacon and a mango. All for only 5,190 colones, a bit steep by my standards.

We arrived back home already drenched and ready for a swim, only to find the keys were no longer in my bag. Our landlady was at the door with the new tank of gas, so she had the privilege of watching our frenzied search in the bag for the key-that-was-not-there.

The gas stove had stopped working last night just as we started to cook dinner, so we were eager to have the stove hooked up. Unfortunately, Colocha was unable to get the tank to attach properly. We must wait for Mauricio to return—he'll be home from work at 1:30 pm.

I promised Colocha I would hunt down the missing keys, so after a few minute's breather, we headed back toward town, hoping to catch our first public bus ride. None of us were in any shape to make the walk again. Besides, the chain was still off the wayward bicycle. The bus was great. It got us there in five minutes flat for only 600 colones.

We had made a list of where we went earlier in the morning...the Pulperia, the Farmacia, the Jungle Café, the roadside stands, Buen Precio—and proceeded to retrace our steps on foot, asking everyone in sight if they had found a set of house keys. The answer was the same everywhere—No, not here...Sorry, can't help you...

Finally, we settled down at Jammin', one of the famous beachfront restaurants that serves a delicious Jamaican jerk chicken. 'Twas a heavenly meal, and the kids even asked for more! Next, a stop at the coral reef on the beach near the police station. Today, I noticed one officer was busy hanging his laundry on the clothesline, and the other was burning some debris in the back lot. There doesn't seem to be much need for an active police force here. But I admit, this is the first time I've seen either one of the officers out of the hammock. The police station is in a prime location, beachfront, with a good breeze going all day long.

Today we spotted a school of 'Nemo' clown fish swimming

through the reef and it was hard to pry Douglas away from the waterfront when it was time to go. Luckily, he soon spotted his sister near the road petting one of the five caballos that had wandered up to munch on the trees in the park. Sweet docile creatures, these small horses wander the town freely. We frequently see them on the beach, in the parks, walking down the roadway with us, and taking a bath every morning in the river that feeds to the oceanfront.

When we arrived home, Mauricio kindly allowed us to keep the spare set of keys until we could arrange for a ride into BriBri where the only key-cutting machine in the area is located. He put the new piece on the stove and for dinner we cooked some rice with the juice of the coconuts brought back from the beach earlier in the day. *Que deliciouso!*

In lieu of television, we've started watching a DVD every night. Tonight, it was Black Beauty and Douglas put himself to bed before the end. Alex, however, sat up a while longer, her half of the malaria prophylaxis in hand, trying hard to muster the courage to swallow it whole. This task seems to become easier and easier for the kids every week and is yet another milestone in their transformation. It is amazing what can be accomplished when a no-nonsense attitude is adopted. You MUST take the pill or you will spend days in the hospital in Limon...

Chapter 6.
Life in the Tropics

June 13th—Second Entry

When we wake up in the morning, the air is cool and the living room just right. We sit in the rocking chairs watching the birds as we breakfast. The kids have identified many species already in the wildlife book, their favorite being the 'house wren' who has made her nest in the eaves high above the breakfast table. We watch her fly back and forth every morning with food for her babies and then listen to the crazed cheeping of these poor little starving creatures as she arrives in the nest with the next worm.

By the time we leave the house, *normally by 7:00 am*, it's a bit sticky. When we arrive back home, by 10 am, we are drenched in sweat. From 10 am to 4 pm, we are drenched in sweat. About 4:00 it starts to cool off; and this is the best time to take a swim, as the sun is starting to go down. We've learned that the beach must be visited before 10 am or after 4 pm; otherwise, we do the hot potato dance all the way to the shoreline.

Alex stopped going in the water suddenly when she experienced a bout with sand in the bathing suit. I'm hoping it's just a phase, but she seems content to lie in the shade on her grass mat reading as we enjoy the cool waters. Sometimes she camps out near one of the hermit crab holes and watches him peek in and out. Her freckles have already melded into one giant mass of freckly across her face and we've all found that the burned shoulders are finally turning to tan. However, since our tans have come from walking into town, rather than lying on the beach, the underside of our arms is now in sharp contract to the top. Nanci suggested a few days ago that Alex and I should take a 'before and after' picture, but I'm afraid it's much too late for that now.

There's a funny little custom around here when walking the road into Puerto. Every few minutes, when a car or more particularly, when a large truck or bus passes, we hold our breath. And close our eyes. There is no way humanly possible to walk into town and come back clean. We now understand the functionality of the lower faucet in the shower. It had seemed an odd thing at first in a shower without a tub. We also use this faucet when washing clothes—at $3 per load for a wash and another $3 per load for a dry, the Laundromat is simply out of the question. I have gathered that their clientele is comprised mainly of tourists.

We're getting to know some of the neighbors. There are familiar faces we pass every morning on our way out. A couple of people who will smile and say 'hola' or the local abbreviation of 'Buenos Dias' every morning. There is the guy from the Ferreteria who sold us the bicycles and has now fixed them on numerous occasions, the man who made a comment in passing about Douglas' broken bicycle chain, and another who put the pedal back on the bicycle the first time it fell off. The lady who sits at the 'packaging' window in the Ferreteria made small talk with me today, yet another breakthrough. I guess we're starting to make it known that we're here to stay.

June 15th

The children are fighting already. It's 7:15 am. I had a discussion yesterday with Nanci regarding enrolling them in the school down in Puerto Viejo. It's a public school where the BriBri children attend. Classes are taught in Spanish, but the teachers all speak English as well, and many of the children speak both languages. We will continue their academic studies in the mornings and evenings at home, but I believe they need the structure, socialization and activities associated with being enrolled in a school. It would also free me up to look for an interim job, perhaps in one of the local hotels or restaurants. The cost of living is not as low as anticipated and we're quickly depleting the modest funds we brought with us.

Jessica, the college girl who is here writing a thesis on Ecotourism, mentioned to me that there is a house on the edge of the jungle where a caretaker lives for room and board. Rumor has it that this man has been stealing from the neighbors and will surely be fired in the next week or so. The job entails a few chores around the yard and house and necessitates being at home every evening after 5 pm. I've thought about inquiring with the owners as to whether they would consider us for the job. I'm told they also provide this man with some food, so an arrangement such as this would be ideal.

Today we will ride into BriBri with Nanci to have the keys cut at the Ferreteria—the hardware store. I'm hoping to also stop in at the grocery and pick up some items that can't be had here in Puerto. We found that juiced limes are particularly tasty and I imagine they will make good Popsicles. We're in need of a Popsicle maker or more likely, a few disposable plastic cups to freeze them in.

A guanabana is the best tasting fruit I've come across yet, but again, there are currently none to be had here in Puerto. We watched Nanci yesterday as she meticulously hand-juiced one of these gigantic, spiky green fruits. This is not an easy task. There are dozens of big black seeds throughout the pulpy center that must be painstakingly squeezed out of individual pods before putting the rest of the fruit in the blender. Nanci explained it's sometimes easier to just 'hand-juice' the guanabana than to try to blend it.

June 15th Second Entry

Jessica came by this afternoon and asked us if we would like to go on a hike Monday with Daniel as guide. She had been asked by another BriBri man if she would like a guide into the Rainforest, but Mauricio explicitly told her it would not be a good idea to go with the other man. I believe the girl is a bit leery of Daniel as well, so maybe we'll accompany her. I love the prospect of another hike through the Rainforest, particularly with my friend Daniel as guide, but if it's the same hike I was treated to during my stay in March, I feel certain the kids will not make it.

The Ferreteria—Everything Has a System... Nanci kindly took us into BriBri again today. This time to have the duplicate keys to the house made. The Ferreteria is an interesting place. They have a *system* and it's the same in each Ferreteria or *hardware store*. First, you walk in, go to the middle of the store and wait at the counter for someone to notice you and decide it's your turn. Then, you explain what you need to purchase; and the item is brought out and shown to you, sometimes by two or three people. Occasionally, its use will be demonstrated as well. *And you must try not to laugh—this is serious business!* A ticket is hand written out if you decide to make the purchase. At that point, you take the ticket to the cajero—the cashier, usually located at the rear of the store. The glass cashier's window with the little hole in the bottom is where you must pay, and a printed receipt rubber-stamped with 'cancelado' is pushed toward you. From there, you must backtrack to the lady sitting at the packing station near the front entrance. Your item magically appears on the counter—in this case, a knife-sharpening stone. She will then take it out of the packaging and meticulously wrap or bag it for you. But first, you must show the printed receipt with the 'cancelado' stamp. Each step must be followed, or you will be told, "No, you must go back to that window."

I find the ways here more amusing than annoying. It seems everything has a process that simply must be followed. In sharp contrast to the ultra-professionalism one experiences while shopping, the Ticos and Caribbean folks are actually some of the most laid-back I've ever met.

Mauricio's mannerism is very interesting. So calm, every word spoken in a soft voice, everything taken in stride. I think Nanci mentioned to me some time ago that all of the BriBri people are like that. No chance of high blood pressure there. I envy them the ability to accept life as it comes and just shrug off anything resembling adversity.

Another calm night here. So many sounds all around us—night sounds. To me, it's the most relaxing time of the day. It's typically cool, sometimes breezy. The sounds of the neighborhood fill the air. Children in the distance, people talking, Caribbean music, the wash of the waves against the shore—all meld together with the sounds of nature.

We spotted a Basilisk lizard the other day. This species is large, about the size of a formidable cat. It startled us when it got up on its hind legs and started running across the yard. I'm told the ability to scurry across rivers in this fashion has earned the Basilisk the nickname of the 'Jesus Christ' lizard.

And the find of the day seems to be the Starfish. Not quite as prevalent as the dozens of sand dollars that are underfoot every few steps, but we have been coming across one every other day or so. You can feel their spiney arms underneath your feet and they are easily picked up with your toes for closer inspection. The starfish here seem to all have nine long legs with a smaller center body, in contrast to the stubby five-point starfish that can be found along the Florida shorelines. The one we found yesterday had been growing back part of a leg that he/she/it must have lost in some mishap or another. A starfish is notorious for it's ability to regenerate from any part of it's body. If a leg is lost, another leg is grown. And interestingly, another body will grow on the severed leg. One starfish becomes two.

Nanci related an interesting story about a small coastal community somewhere in the world that was overrun by starfish. The locals, at a loss as to how to deal with the problem, first tried to poison them. When the poison didn't work, everyone in the community went down to the waterfront and chopped up the starfish with machetes. *Little did they know....*

June 16th

Bicycles gone bad...it is evident to us now that the two children's bicycles that we purchased are—you guessed it— pieces of *@(%^&. The story I had been told about the bicycles here being Extremely Sturdy was a *fabrication* of the highest magnitude. My bicycle is pretty sturdy, being of the one-piece frame, coaster brake, cruiser sort. Not so for the children. And broken bicycles make for frustration—lots of it. Something about the way the tires took three tries to inflate, and the way the overall alignment looked a bit askew, should have tipped me off when we were making the original purchase, but they WERE *very cheap* and the reality of it was that the kids simply could not mount the larger sturdier model.

Today it was Alex's turn to experience the dismay of a bicycle falling apart, piece-by-piece, as she rode down the gravel road. It all started last night, when suddenly her front wheel froze where it was, instantly and with no warning, flipping her halfway up into the air. Good thing she was pushing it though the front gate at the time—and not riding it.

I spent hours with the bicycle upside down on the grass; I took off every nut, every bolt, completely reconstructed the front brakes. Still nothing. This morning, the front wheel began to turn a bit when forced, so we decided to chance a trip to the Ferreteria. After having the tire reinflated, I bought our very own bicycle pump (which has since broken) and we were on our way toward town.

The Big Scare... Down into Puerto to check email we went, with Douglas in the lead. In fact, with Alex whining about the quality of her ride, and stopping every few minutes to stomp her feet, Douglas soon disappeared from sight. *No worries—he'll stop at the intersection at the entrance to town*...Problem was, when we reached the intersection, my child was nowhere in sight. Visions of America's Most Wanted horror stories crashed through my *mente* as I frantically shouted his name. Then Alex, quietly by my side, made a profound statement. *He is probably at the Internet Café, Mommy*...Surely, this little person wouldn't have made his way through still unfamiliar territory, all the way to the Jungle Café. The thought seemed inconceivable to me. We hurriedly made our way toward the Café with hearts pounding, and lo and behold, up he bounded. *Mom, we're in luck—they're just opening!* Naturally, Douglas had gone on to our destination, then sat on the curb patiently waiting for us to arrive...

Bicycle woes... As we left the Jungle Café, and turned the corner onto the main drag, Alex started complaining about her bicycle once again. She soon stopped short and refused to go any further, so Douglas and I proceeded down the few blocks to make an ATM stop, and *yes, all the while keeping Alex in our sight*. When we got back to where my daughter had stoically held her ground, I realized that we had *real bike problems* here. The wheel was jammed again, so I half-carried the bicycle across the road to the nearest bicycle rental shop. There I was told—No, we don't fix bicycles. Go to the end of town, turn right before the main road, another few blocks in that direction and you will see the shop on your right. Ask for Gallo...

Still half dragging the bicycle with the front-wheel-that-would-not-turn, we started in the direction of the mysterious 'Gallo'. A few seconds later, the entire front wheel actually *fell off*. I then carried the bicycle, the wheel, and sundry small parts from the brakes that were beginning to disintegrate, the rest of the way. It was well past 10:00 by then; and I was not a happy camper.

We found the bicycle repairman after two more stops to ask directions to his shop, and were told *"This is not good—this part is bad."* Pointing to the front axle. No kidding. *"Regresa en una hora."* Come back in an hour.

We made the best of the hour by trying out yet another local restaurant, this time for breakfast. For me, the meal was a scrumptious plate of gallo pinto (rice with black beans) with eggs, cheese and toast. And of course, a glass of my favorite guanabana juice con agua. For the kids, there was a plate-size pancake with ice cream on top. Weird, but true. It turned out to be orange sherbet. Alex turned up her nose when she saw that it was orange, and not 'plain' vanilla ice cream. Luckily, Douglas had ordered his pancake 'solo'. Both kids balked at the pancakes as they were served because they were a bit over-brown, and proceeded to dig out the middle portion— between the top and the bottom layer of the pancake. Since this was not the first such incident, I've been subsisting on the kid's leftovers for the past week.

The bicycle was finally finished. The front tire was properly inflated, and it sported a shiny new front axle. Only 1500 colones for the job—about $3.15. Maybe I should take the receipt to the *Ferreteria* and challenge the quality of their merchandise. In great spirits then, we decided to take the only road south—toward Manzanillo. We made it as far as Charlie's Place, an outdoor café located just north of Cocles, where we collapsed and ordered more drinks. I can honestly say I've been spending more on liquid than food since we arrived here. But after the 24-hour bout the second day after our arrival, when Douglas suddenly stopped peeing, hydration is now high on the list of Must-Dos.

Alex's back tire of course went flat before we got home— three times. The pump we purchased this morning at the Ferreteria fell apart. So she continued to ride it flat. Stopping only on occasion to stomp her feet and snarl. We make quite a spectacle at times. *Only American children act like this*, I'm told, and my observations tend to concur. The indigenous BriBri children play all the time, smiling, and when one of them gets hurt accidentally, they just keep on playing. There is no whining, no punching the other guy back. And the local Tico children—well, I suspect that parental discipline here is the way it was in our grandparent's day…

Headaches in Paradise…We had a long day today downtown—in the sun, followed by a couple of hours on the beach, until Alex announced that she had a headache. It's hard not to panic when one hears the word 'headache'. I've done my research…*Dengue. Sudden onset headache…excruciating, blinding pain. Progresses rapidly…must seek medical attention with first onset of symptoms…*

Many of you will be surprised to hear this—but yes, my little Alex is a Drama Queen. She exhibited every symptom of sudden-onset dengue, then laid down for a blissfully quiet hour (during which I checked her pulse every five minutes). Other than being sticky from napping mid-afternoon, she seemed fine. She woke up and immediately resumed bickering with Douglas, so I think it is safe to assume that *Alex does not have dengue.*

I did find out though, that the nearest full-service clinic is actually in BriBri, a short drive up the mountain—*for those who own a car.* The clinic here in Puerto is open evening hours, 4:30 pm to 8:00 pm and staffed as a courtesy by the local Minister of Health. The same Minister of Health who recently offered to see any of 'Nanci's' children for free. In the event of an emergency, an ambulance can be summoned to the Hone Creek clinic, and on to Limon if necessary.

Ah, the peace of *late* evening. Children are in bed. Surrounded by darkness and the now-familiar night sounds. The waves, the night-bugs, the funny little chirping house lizards. Someone is burning a fire tonight. And the stars are out, clear and crisp in the flawless sky…another perfect ending.

Chapter 7.
The Stars Begin to Shift

June 17th

Bad days never last... Somehow in the grand scheme of things, memories of a *bad day* seem to fade quickly. Today was a good day. We went to the Ferreteria to purchase another attachment for the bicycle pump, then stopped at Barry and Nanci's to pick up our fruit and veggie order. The veggie truck passes by El Puente at 6:00 am on Friday mornings, and we were looking forward to the goodies it would yield. Waiting for us was a large bag of potatoes, pineapple, mango, and a handful of juicy limes and lemons.

Another trip to Limon... When we arrived, we were greeted by Barry who announced that Nanci was just about to leave for Limon and had been looking for some company. Not sure whether this was really the case, at least the part about wanting company. But in any event, Nanci graciously offered to take us with her. The kids are getting the hang of how things work around here. *It's much better to ride than to walk, and if you fight in the car, that person will never, ever take you in their car again...*They were amazingly docile on the ride to

Limon, and were rewarded with the first pizza we've had since our arrival.

Nanci and I found halter-tops at a street vendor for 500 colones, a little over a dollar each, and I picked up several packages of the coveted boiled ham and hot dogs that are hard to find down our way. A side trip to BriBri to pick up Saturday's food bolsas yielded more homemade sweet bread at the Panaderia and a long loaf of fresh Cuban-style bread. We stopped again on the return trip to pick up bananas from the BriBri woman at her roadside stand. This woman has taken out a small loan, and each time Nanci stops to purchase her bananas there, the loan is reduced by that amount.

Landslides are scary things... The landslide on the way to BriBri seemed a bit more prominent this morning and Nanci noted that several people she knows have lost relatives to this natural occurrence over the years, one as recently as three weeks ago. It seems everything here is taken in stride, even death. It's treated as just-one-of-those-things-that-happens and is viewed much more as a natural part of the life cycle, than something to be dreaded and feared as it is in some other parts of the world.

June 18th

The Saturday 'Mercado'... This morning we decided to go down to the *mercado* in Puerto. It opens up at 7:30 am and typically everything is gone by 10:00 am. I'd heard from several people that there would be items for sale there that cannot be had in the local grocery store. *Chocolate* for example. We picked up several pieces of sweet organic dark chocolate, some homemade yogurt made by a local Amish family—one strawberry and the other a pineapple-banana medley—and a few slices of banana-nut bread. The purchases were well worth the hours wait at the bus stop this morning, only to have the bus fly past us, leaving us in it's dust. We had walked into Puerto, grumbling all the way, but the stars suddenly shifted and we were fortunate enough to catch the northbound for the return trip. *Adonde? La pulperia violetta...*

Where are you going? The purple store...600 colones please. Never mind that we had to stand. The bus is a luxury we've learned to appreciate.

Getting acquainted... Today was our second Soup Kitchen day and the BriBri people are starting to get to know us. Many of the faces are familiar and I noticed one woman who showed up seemed to be a 'new one,' someone I had never seen before. Douglas had a major embarrassing moment when he inadvertently asked one of the older women if she wanted to 'go searching for animals' with him, rather than "Would you like some more coffee?" A mix of indignation and surprise crossed the poor woman's face briefly until she realized he had simply mixed up his words. Then he was 'cute' drawing smiles and pats on the head.

Yesterday, I turned around, ready to head toward the house, and Douglas had taken off up the path into the Rainforest with Alejandro—in his short pants and flip-flops. Of course, Alejandro was barefoot. He's a pretty jungle-wise kid, I'm told. I believe the words Nanci used were *"Well, he's lived in the jungle all his life, and hasn't been eaten by a Boa yet, so Douglas will be just fine with Alejandro."* Sure made me feel a lot better.

Embarrassing moments... The key to fitting in here is letting go of any and all stress. That is hard to do when your child is throwing a full-blown temper tantrum because he can't get the sheets to fold properly on his bed...and you know every neighbor within a mile around can hear him. *There are no walls that separate.* First thing this morning, we had just such an incident. Mauricio, our landlord, approached us later when he spotted us at the mercado and asked Douglas if everything was ok now. *Que verguenza!* Talk about embarrassing moments. The fact that Mauricio addressed us with the words "Hello, family!" made me feel a *little bit* better.

June 18th Second Entry

Of Crabs and Tarantulas... Those of you who know me know that I *occasionally* tend to get wrapped up in a project, whatever project it may be at the moment, in what some would refer to as an *intensely obsessive way*. It is in this way that Alex and I managed to purge a bulging bolsa full of clothing this evening—to be donated to the people who live up in the Rainforest. We kept an entire trunk full of 'cool weather' clothing, and another trunk full of 'wearable' clothing. Who knows when we might venture into other parts of the country where the temperature ranges 72 F year-round? (Remind me again why we are HERE, where it is a continual 86 deg plus with a heat index of 96 deg plus).

As my young daughter and I dumped trunk after trunk of clothing onto the bed, Douglas ran around the house, as is his evening custom, chasing lizards and oversized butterflies. By the time we were done, he had brought in a fist-sized hard-shelled crab that he *says* he found in the yard. The thing was kept in a large metal cooking pot until the three of us decided we could not bear to boil it alive, as had been the original intent. So Douglas set out to let it go free. As he lifted the lid, it went free all right—in the kitchen. It went scurrying behind piled trunks, underneath the countertop gas stove, and finally, cornered with it's back against the wall, in the fighting stance. It continued backing up and snapping its pincers every time we got near it. We finally managed to shoo it out the front door with the help of the broom and it quickly ran down the nearest hole. *Sigh! So much for that seafood dinner...*

I'd really rather not think too much about the second adventure of this 'late' evening—since I'll be going to bed soon in the room in which it was found—*and squashed*. It was fuzzy, gray, and much resembled a Tarantula. We're not entirely sure, as it was *squashed quickly* and thus rendered unidentifiable. Douglas had seen a Tarantula up close in his classroom last year and he was SURE that is what we had here. It was crawling up the trunk near the wall in my bedroom. *That is why I'm still downstairs and not in the bed.* Not sure how long I'll sit here, but the hammock looks somewhat inviting at the moment.

Before the kids retired for the night, the *unknown spider species* sighting necessitated an extra thumping of the mattresses. It's a thing we do every night that makes us feel falsely secure. We pick up the 3" thick mattress and thump it down hard on the bed. Then we shake the gecko poop off of the sheets and hit the pillows down hard. Just to be sure. Tuck in the edges of the mosquito netting, check *inside the netting* for mosquitoes...then we go to sleep. Sometimes sleep comes quickly. Exhaustion has a way of doing that to you. And sometimes it does not come so quickly. I have a feeling tonight will be one of those nights.

June 18th Much later...

Life is full of choices. We can choose Corn Flakes or Shredded Wheat for breakfast. Goth or conservative dress. Mariah Carey or George Jones. And we can choose to live in Fear or not to live in Fear. This being said, I choose NOT to live in Fear. As I lay down tonight underneath my mosquito netting, I began to let Fear get the best of me. The sounds on the roof, the sounds underneath, creaking all around. The shadows on the wide-open windows. The boogeyman who might be lurking. The arachnids that might crawl up *underneath my net.*

Heart pounding. Adrenaline pumping. Then, the conscious choice not to choose Fear. My pulse is visibly more even now. The waves are washing over the shore lulling me into the unconscious dream state. Fear—something that never crossed my range of emotions—from the time I first decided to take this Adventure, up to this very moment—*Fear* almost got the best of me tonight.

June 19th

The Great Hunter... Everyone knows that Douglas is a born hunter. From the time he started to totter around on baby feet, Douglas has hunted...geckos, butterflies, insects of every imaginable shape, size and color. He is rarely seen without his butterfly net and snake boots. Sometimes now he dons the khaki safari hat and much resembles the boy in the movie 'The Blue Butterfly'. Today was the greatest catch of his young life. I heard the yelp first and saw the red throbbing thumb and forefinger after the fact. Then again—another yelp followed by a resonating *"I Got Him!!!!"* echoing endlessly across the deserted beach. *Blue Crab.* About fist-size, just enough for a meal. Well, a meal for one.

The crab caught earlier in the yard had turned out to be a non-edible dirt crab, a disgusting looking creature that turns one's stomach at the very thought of consuming it. Colocha warned "Do not eat this one—he eats dirt," as she pointed to the dirt pouch hanging from the underside of it's body. But the beach crab, now he was another story. Running freely on the sandy beaches, spotlessly clean, and *very* tasty looking...Alex shut the door and curled up on the hammock as we cooked it, but she later broke apart the small claws and hand-fed the succulent meat to Douglas. The Great Hunter has brought home a *Buena Comida...*

Chopping or Shopping? I'm pretty sure I made an *Error* today. A small man with one squinty eye started a conversation with me as we were bicycling toward town this morning. He was walking in the same direction. *Where do you live? Where do you work? Do you want to go 'chopping' with me tomorrow? 7 am sharp. Ok, then, have a good day...*Shopping, at 7 am? Strange request. After the fact, I realized with much dismay that he must have been a *Chapear* and he, in fact, had been asking me if I needed my lawn cut. A C*hapear* is a man with a machete— the local version of a lawn mower. He'll be showing up here at 7 am tomorrow morning. Only problem is I don't own this house and have no authority to hire a *Chapear.*...Uh, oh.

When It Rains It Pours... The waves were what tipped me off. Normally gentle and rolling, the waves breaking near the shore topped four to five feet this afternoon, sweeping me off my feet in knee-deep water. As I faced the sea, I had a terrible uncanny flash as to the collective terror that must have been felt as the tsunami in Asia brought in the crashing Giant Wave. Amazing thing—the sea. Today so tumultuous, churning in every direction. Other days, so gentle, much like the lick of a kitten.

We had wanted to see the movie...Castaway, starring Tom Hanks. It was showing down at Charlie's Place. Barry mentioned it the other day, but since I hadn't heard back from him, we decided to make our way alone. Even living less than a mile away, communication is oft times difficult without a telephone.

We managed to catch the southbound bus, but it only went as far as downtown Puerto. From there, we walked a block further, through what seemed a seedier section of town. With each passing moment, the deserted stretch of roadway to the south looked less and less inviting.

A change of plans was in order, so we stopped again at Jammin' for some more of their delicious jerk chicken. Today the waiter was a young Panamanian, recently relocated from Bocas del Toro. Engrossed in a conversation with two female tourists, they quickly convinced him to sing a little Reggae. The man had a beautiful voice, deep and rich, full of the heart of the Caribbean. He explained to the tourists that he had once recorded a few CDs, and then something or other prevented him from going further with his career. He works a second job at Reggae Night held once a week at one of the local bars.

The dark clouds turned to rain before we left Jammin' and we started out toward the house with dampened spirits. By the time we reached the bus stop a few blocks away, it was pouring. We sat for a long time. Some local teens who had consumed a little too much cerveza kept us entertained by chasing the giant crabs that were washing to the surface of the roadway. Douglas would shine the flashlight on a crab, then one of the inebriated young men would go after it. One sees a free childlike spirit in the people here. Even the dismay of being stuck under a tin roof overhang with a deluge all around was not viewed by any other than us as a tragedy.

It became evident that there would be no more bus tonight.

It was 8:30 pm and a Sunday. As the time crept toward 9:00 pm, I decided we had no other choice but to walk home. The kids were falling asleep on the bench and were unnerved by the lightning and crashes of thunder all around. As we started on our way, we passed another small shelter. A voice from within asked us if we'd been unable to catch a taxi. *Mauricio is everywhere.* I wonder at times if he's actually looking out for us, as he seems to turn up in the most unusual places. He was leaning against the post in his familiar relaxed stance, his dark skin blending into the night. I never would have seen him there.

Lucky for us, Mauricio explained that the taxis here are mostly Piratas—unmarked private cars. They are the cars with the little blue or red flashing strobe lights in the windows, the ones we've seen all evening, pulling up to the curb, then speeding away. Cell phones ringing. We went back to the bus shelter and with Mauricio's help, soon caught a ride home. The cost? One-thousand colones, a little over $2.00. As it turns out, a taxi is not as out-of-the-question as I had thought.

The casita really felt like home now, a comforting place, shelter from the storm. We woke up at 4 am with wind whipping through the windows, slamming the shutters, trees creaking all around. This morning there were little bug pellets everywhere. I guess they blew down off the roof or the eaves in the wind. Seems the rain washes everything clean, even the inside of the house. So we swept, starting at the top and going toward the bottom level. Shook everything out. And swept again. I reminded the kids that it would be much easier if they kept their toys in the plastic trunks that we brought with us. That way an event such as this would not take as much cleanup time after the fact.

Chapter 8.
Oh, No! What Have I Done?

June 20th

Frustration, Depression, and a General Malaise... Barry pulled up in his car from behind and we spoke through the open window. He said just about now is when I should begin to experience the feeling that generally equates to *"What in the world have I done?"* Perhaps he had observed from a distance the weight of depression that I had been carrying along with me all day or maybe it is simply such a common occurrence that it's easy to gauge in us newcomers. I had known it would come; everything I read about relocating overseas had prepared me for the onset. Now that it has settled in around me, I don't quite know what to do with it.

There are therapeutic ways commonly practiced in this region. Healing arts, spiritual healing; many are deep into the metaphysical.

> *The crashing of the waves had a calming effect on me. I stood mesmerized by the ocean's edge this evening. Fascinated by every rise and fall of the high tide. The sea is again tumultuous and has a mysterious hint of danger lurking*

just beneath its surface. I can't seem to draw myself away once I am captured by it. Even now, back at the house, the crashing of the waves envelopes us. Maybe this is part of the healing.

Warm Fuzzies from Friends... It seems I am loved. And today was the day I needed it most. God has a way of touching us and of making it known that He is here, watching out for us in ways we never imagined—even when we conveniently forget He is there. I received confirmation of God's presence in our lives as I opened my emails this afternoon. There were many of them—forty-seven to be exact. I was overwhelmed with emotion at all of the caring that overflowed as I opened each one. The presence of friends, even in such a faraway place, is comforting. It's good to know we are not forgotten.

Chapter 9.
The Adventure Continues...

June 21st

It is interesting to watch the dynamics between Douglas and his new friends. He and Alejandro, a ten year-old BriBri boy have hit it off, although Douglas is just-turned-seven and closer in age to William, Alejandro's younger brother. Seems the intellectual connection is there for them though.

The four siblings are a close-knit group. Carmelita, probably eleven or twelve, fast approaching the age at which her mother gave birth to her—age fourteen. Maria, just eight and the picture of innocence. Huge brown eyes and a smile that stretches the expanse of her beautiful brown face. Alejandro, the curious one. Smart as a whip, learning to use computers at 'The Bridge' in a culture where technology is considered 'taboo'. And little William, an extension of his older brother, a little shy, a little leery of these white strangers and their direct ways.

Since day one, Alejandro and Douglas have gone off on their own to *buscar animales*—search for animals—with wildlife guides in hand. Every chance they get, they can be found together. This newfound friendship has thrown to the wind everything the original 'foursome' has ever known. While swimming with the children last Friday, Carmelita and William hung back as Douglas and Alejandro played. Maria and Alex swam in unison, but more in a side-by-side fashion than together. *Then they discovered the sand.*

William and Maria play with Douglas in the sand

I've been told that although the BriBri children have been attending swim lessons for the past few months, they had never actually *played* in the sand. And the beginning of the swim lessons was the first time in their lives they had actually stepped into the water...Strange to imagine in children who have grown up a stone's throw from the sea's edge. Alejandro giggled as he rolled down the sloping ledge recently formed by the waves, all the way into the frothy water. He and Douglas dug a moat with mounds of sand piled on each side. Alex quickly joined in and did what she does best—directed the construction that the boys were involved in. By the time we left the beach that day, all six children were actively involved in the sand-play, with perhaps another small step behind us in our journey toward understanding.

June 22nd

Dilemma on the Bus... How do you say, *"Your chicken is dripping on my daughter?"* in Patois? Undoubtedly, we had a dilemma. The elderly black couple sitting in front of us on the bus back from Limon had stowed what appeared to be a whole chicken wrapped in a plastic bag, up above them. It was thawing quickly. Every time the bus hit a bump, a droplet of condensation—or chicken blood—we're not really sure, came flying back and hit Alex on the knees. *Mommy, I think it's a chicken. Yup, it looks like a chicken...Ask them to move it...Well, I would if I could, but I have not a clue as to how to even begin a conversation with them. Do you hear them speaking? It's not Spanish, is it mommy?*

So every other stop or so, I nonchalantly stood up and pushed the chicken up a little further—until it was sitting squarely above the woman's head. Needless to say, it soon began to drip on her. Alex and I fought hard to keep our giggling under control as the scene unfolded...A droplet here and there, which the woman brushed away. This soon followed by the realization of what was happening. Then, a loud, animated conversation with her husband. The man quickly retrieved the chicken and stowed it at his feet.

June 22nd Second Entry

New Bicycle Repairman... Yesterday was my turn for bicycle problems. My bike undoubtedly had a flat. I had a feeling it was a 'permanent' flat and not the type of flat that can be fixed by simply putting more air in the tire. This was confirmed as we got about twenty meters down the gravel road and found the tire was flat again.

About this time, the chapear with the one squinty eye appeared from somewhere on the beach and chivalrously pumped up the tire for me. I found out later that his apparent Good Samaritan efforts are common practice in this region; however, I've been unknowingly neglecting one important thing—tipping the man each time he comes to my rescue.

Our destination was the Steven's house where I was hoping

to perhaps find a competent male who could handle the repair for me. Of course, we stopped along the way to provide our daily financial support to the local Ferreteria, where I purchased a new inner tube for the damaged tire.

Daniel, the BriBri man who works for the Stevens, was still in the process of constructing a new chicken coop for Chicken McNugget. McNugget is the orphaned peep quickly turned full-grown chicken rescued by Nanci from a local vet's office.

Daniel said he knew someone who could fix the bicycle for me, and wheeled it across the street to a neighbor's house. As it turns out, Abel is a handy young man who operates a fix-it shop out of his front yard just across the road from El Puente. His mother also sells homemade ice cream to the local children for 50 colones apiece. She offers all of the usual flavors—pineapple, banana, and my all-time favorite—guanabana. The only qualm I had about the ice cream was when I spotted two chickens wandering freely in and out of the house.

Quince minutos Daniel said. The bicycle will be ready in 15 minutes. When I asked Abel how much I owed him, he shrugged and said whatever I wanted to give him. I handed him a 1000 colones bill, a little less than the shop in town had charged me, but probably more that he had been expecting. His expression said it was an agreeable exchange.

Douglas and the unknown bite…Douglas was doing his usual exploring this evening when he was bitten by something from inside a hollow PVC pipe laying in front of the house. We were all sure we saw 'fang' marks on his pinkie finger, when he declared the pain in the finger was creeping into his hand, and then to his lower arm. It's hard to tell with Douglas. It could have been a spider, maybe a small scorpion, probably not a snake. Ten minutes had elapsed and the finger was not red, nor was it turning black. But Douglas *was very sure* he saw a black tail slither away under the house…What to do?

Luckily, Mauricio and Colocha appeared to be home this

evening so I decided to play it safe and take Douglas into town to the clinic. We readied quickly and met Mauricio at the lower level of his home. Would he mind calling us a taxi? *We need to go to the clinic.* Mauricio pulled Douglas up under the light and examined his finger. "Go home and put ice on it," he said. Surely it's not a snake, and with a scorpion bite, the child would be still crying. So we rethought a taxi ride into town, went home, iced the finger again, and within ten minutes, he was miraculously cured. *Always good to get a second opinion...*

Chapter 10.
Adjusting to Life in the Tropics

June 23rd

Pan Tostada... We found a great new product this week and have been buying it in bulk ever since. Crispy, crunchy, buttery tasting...Toast. Yesterday, during our trip to Limon, the shiny glint of appliances through a storefront window caught our attention. Once inside, we realized why most people here do not have *electrodomesticas*. A small blender cost over 25,000 colones—in excess of $50.00 US. A bit steep for someone who makes on average 700 colones per hour. Besides, Nanci told me she has gone through two blenders and four juicers in the year and a half she has been living here. The climate apparently is not conducive to electrodomesticas.

Living on Tico Time... After the first week, I noticed my indestructible, waterproof to 1,000 feet, titanium watch was beginning to erode. Large pits covered the backside of the watch and the edges were looking a bit like Swiss cheese. Another few days, and one of the little buttons had fallen off. Our two-week anniversary marked the day that the watch was found to be D.O.A. when we arose in the morning. We are now living on 'Tico' time, which happens to be whenever one gets around to doing a thing. Maybe today, maybe tomorrow, could be next week...*no hurries, no worries.*

Future possibilities...I had a conversation with Jeffrey today. The epitome of the Caribbean, Jeffrey is the guy with the dreadlocks who owns the corner store, and apparently also owns a long stretch of land along the highway across from Playa Negra. The land was inherited from his father and has since been divided amongst he and his brothers. Jeffrey took me out behind the store, and I was surprised to step from the chaotic noisy storefront to a serene *patio* with two crisp white Caribbean-style houses set far back into the manicured lawn. We discussed my current rent, and the obvious advantage to purchasing a piece of land and building a small house. Only a two-minute walk across the road to the endless isolated black sand beach, it seems to me the land has the potential of increasing in value.

We talked about houses. Wood houses, concrete houses, two-story houses. I asked Jeffrey to give me an estimate on a basic one-story. He drew me out a sketch of such a house, along with a description of the types of materials used in construction. The end result sounded pretty reasonable. Amenities, such as a screen porch could always be added on later down the road. So options are opening up for us, although we are a long way from making such a commitment.

June 24th
Clinic Saga—Day One
La Clinica... The Clinic in Hone Creek was reminiscent of the hospital scene in the movie 'The Blue Butterfly' which was filmed just up the road near BriBri. Maybe it was the same place. Tuesday morning, I woke up to find two large reddened patches of skin on my upper legs. They felt akin to sunburn and within a day, the one on the left was blistering as well. After showing this affliction to numerous Americanos, it was decided that a trip to the clinic would be the prudent thing to do.

The *clinic saga* began yesterday afternoon. Barry drove me

to Hone Creek and graciously offered to 'show me the ropes'. It's a bit of a confusing process, as is everything unfamiliar. We made our way toward the back of the open-air building where Barry held a conversation in broken Spanish with the cashier at the emergency room window. He gave her the name of the doctor I wanted to see, and it was not until later that we understood the odd look that crossed her face. The doctor that Barry was accustomed to asking for when he brings in the BriBri children is evidently a pediatrician who only sees children less than ten years of age.

Next, we waited. There were only two or three other people in the entire building, and of course, the lady who perpetually pushes the floor-waxing machine, and the birds, flitting through every few minutes to look for a few crumbs. A glance up toward the eaves revealed several nests, mostly belonging to the local wren species that are seen in almost every building. Near the front entrance to the door, a collection of old bottles sits high up on a shelf. They initially appear to be nothing more than a batch of cleaning products. Upon closer inspection, the bottles reveal several pickled snakes, ranging from long, skinny vipers to colorful variations of the coral snake. Could it be they were caught slithering through the hallways?

After a few more inquiries of the passing staff members, I was finally called back to see *el medico*. Since it was after 4 pm, I had not been lucky enough to see the black doctor who speaks English. My doctor was completely Spanish speaking, rattling off more than I could process at one time. In the end, it was decided that what I had were *picaduras de arana*—spider bites. Seemed a bit odd to me since there were no visible bites or punctures, just the strange redness seeming to come from inside my skin. He prescribed two crèmes and an injection of antihistamine. Also, I must come back in the morning for lab tests to check the coagulation of my blood, and oh, don't forget to pay the cashier tomorrow, as she is now closed. *Is it really possible that the Honor System continues to live in this secluded corner of the world? I never cease to be amazed at the odd mix of the old and the new that can be found here.*

Clinic Saga—Day Two

Today, we arose at 6:55 am—too late to catch the 7:15 bus to the clinic. So we walked up to the bus stop, and eventually toward Hone Creek in hopes of flagging down the bus midway.

The morning at the clinic was a long one, exacerbated perhaps by the fact that the kids were with me this time. The first stop was the lab window to have my blood drawn; and I was handed a baby food jar with a rusty top for what I assumed was a urine specimen. Could not help but wonder how accurate the test would turn out. The bathroom was a bit unkempt for a hospital. Plastic seats were missing on the toilets and there was no running water in the sink. *This was not exactly a good thing for someone trying to pee into a baby food jar.* Douglas announced that the men's room had running water, so I boldly walked in there to wash my hands.

About an hour and a half, the technician told me. So we sat on the wooden bench next to a local *policia*. Douglas was terrified for some reason; and he kept shooting the policeman 'looks' which caused the man to smirk every so often. By the time his turn was called, the *policia* had conversed with several small children sitting behind us, and also rumpled the hair on Alex's baby doll that sat in her lap. Not as tough as they look.

The prescription window yielded two tubes of crème. Since there was no request for money, I assumed these were included in the 16,000 colones for the ER visit—about $30 for someone with no insurance. I noticed the name on the larger tube of crème started with the letters S.U.L.F.A. Last time I had taken sulfa pills for another ailment, my tongue had shredded and swollen to twice its normal size. I assume this means I'm allergic. I brought this to the attention of the pharmacist. *Un momento.* He disappeared behind the thick dead-bolted door for about 15-minutes, then reappeared with a smile. No problem, the crème is ok to use *even if you are allergic to Sulfa.*

My name was called at the lab window after what seemed eons waiting. For some reason, being without a watch is still a bit disturbing to me. I guess I haven't yet adjusted to 'Tico time'. I was handed the lab results and told to go back to the ER. Another wait there, and I was finally seen by the doctor. My luck was beginning to change, as the doctor who speaks English was on duty this time. After a brief look at my legs, he asked if I had made lemonade anytime recently and then gone out in the sun? Hmmm...I *had* made lemonade from the lemons purchased from the fruit truck. Was it Monday, the day before the burns had mysteriously appeared? And I do remember sitting out on the beach that one morning earlier this week, not at our typical beach time, until I felt a bit French-fried. The doctor explained to me that what I most obviously had was a case of extreme sunburn in the spots where I had inadvertently rubbed the acid of the lemons on my legs. He conveniently refused to answer when I mentioned that I had been told by another medico just yesterday that these were spider bites.

So we've learned a thing or two about medical care in our area. The clinic down in Puerto is temporarily closed, as the Health Minister is on a trip to Honduras. The clinic in Hone Creek is passable, but only during the day. However, they do have an ambulance. I pity the person who has to stay in that lonely hospital bed there overnight.

And I understand better Colocha's insistence that everything can be treated the 'natural' way. Few people here trust the clinic and its *doctores* who perhaps never made it completely through their medical training. I felt sorry for the elderly woman sitting on the hard bench in the waiting room this afternoon. She was biting down hard on a washcloth, and appeared to have some kind of acute abdominal pain. I imagine she was the one who had left the bloodied urine specimen on the counter. The road for her will be a long one; hopefully, she will be sent on to the hospital in Limon before whatever affliction she has takes its toll.

Chapter 11.
It's the Little Things...

Afternoon delight... We had a surprise afternoon shower today—right after I hung the day's laundry. No problem, the cool breezes it brought more than compensated for the inconvenience. We realize now why the hammock has been damp every morning. The showers here are punishing, blowing in from every direction. Invariably, tree limbs can be heard crashing to the ground and small flying projectiles are all around. We settled down in the center of the living room, away from the wet zone, and played a couple rounds of UNO. The kids remarked it was fun, just like the hurricane that hit Central Florida last September when the schools were closed down for a week...

It's cool now, 6:12 pm, and the darkness is settling in around us. The kids are making me yet another cup of my favorite vanilla *café* to which I am now quite addicted. Our home is equipped with a 'typical' Tico coffee maker, a basic wooden stand with a 2" diameter hole in the center. They love filling the little hanging 'sock' with fresh grounds, and pouring the hot water through to brew it. Douglas has talked me into allowing him a taste in his very own tin cup. What the heck—I've watched children as young as three offered a cup of afternoon coffee as a matter of course. The novelty was short-lived, as both children found the hot, dark liquid to be extremely distasteful.

The missing Butterfly Net... Today was wrought with disappointment for Douglas. His prized possession, the butterfly net purchased at the Museum of Natural History, has disappeared. It was last seen at the Stevens yesterday afternoon, where he and William were playing during my unexpected trip to the clinic. Today we managed to recover his bag of marbles and safari hat—but the butterfly net was nowhere to be found. I have a feeling it may have gotten up and walked away into the Rainforest...

The kids have already compensated for this Great Loss by constructing a makeshift net. A stick, some surgical tape from the first aid kit, and a shoelace from one of the old useless packed sneakers and wallah...we now have a serviceable, albeit oddly shaped, butterfly net.

The Handmade House... As we passed a neat looking wood board house this afternoon, Barry noted that the owner had built it himself from the ground up. *From the trees growing in his back yard.* This man had cut down the trees, cured the lumber, and then built the house, all with his own two hands. Nothing like the satisfaction of a job well-done.

It seems the skilled trades are most in demand here. People who can fix bicycles, people who can build houses, people who are skilled with a machete. From about tenth grade on, willing students are enrolled in what is the equivalent of a two-year postsecondary trade school, learning everything from construction to engineering skills. Once graduated, they receive their 'Titulos' or titles, and are thus ready to enter the work world.

It's Raining Geckos... Yesterday as I sat on the living room steps reading, I felt a huge *Splat* on my right arm. I assumed it was just one of the 4" black grasshoppers that are in season right now—until I spotted the green gecko on the binding of my book. He had fallen approximately 15 feet from the wall where they play every evening, chasing each other, and avoiding Douglas—who is chasing them. They run in and out of the walls, into the upstairs bedrooms, and back into the living room. Once we are in bed, they begin to chirp and continue throughout the night.

It seems I'm not the only one who has problems with flying creatures. A prehistoric-sized cockroach zoomed a crazy landing pattern around and around Alex this afternoon, before succumbing to a crash landing, smack into her left thigh. It was enough of an impact to bring out the ice pack; we're debating whether a bruise will show up by morning.

June 25th

Douglas the barfing wonder...I had never given a thought to purchasing cleaning products and a mop since our rent includes weekly cleaning of the house. Sweeping the floors daily had seemed sufficient. Until last night...when Douglas appeared at my bedside around 3 am. I could vaguely see his outline in the moonlight as he said the dreaded words, "Mommy, I don't feel good," and proceeded to vomit all over the floor. I grabbed him and pushed his head out the wide-open window, but already my sheets and mosquito netting had been splattered. This was the first time I REALLY missed my washing machine. Middle of the night hand-washing of the sheets, netting, and towels kept us up for quite some time. Once his stomach had settled, my youngest son and I had a nice little chat as we rocked in the wooden chairs in the darkness of the night. It was a good time to bond.

Regalitos... Alex decided this morning that she would like to give Maria one of her Barbie dolls. She meticulously chose one of the six that she had brought with her when we moved, then dressed it in a coordinating outfit. She later decided it might be a good idea to also give a Barbie to Carmelita, Maria's older sister. The gifts were accepted with smiles and *muchas gracias.* Last week when the kids noticed that Maria and Alejandro swam in their underwear, they each picked out one of their own bathing suits to give to them. Funny thing though, after about 15 minutes, Maria had pushed down the pink one-piece suit to expose her entire upper body from bellybutton to neck—the suit soon resembled a pair of underpants around her waist. *Old habits die hard.*

Saturday Mercado... We have gotten into a new routine it seems. On Saturday mornings we head for the bus stop and take the easy way into Puerto to see what we can find at the Mercado. Today we arose a little later than usual, but still managed to get there before all the goodies were gone. More of the little rolls of organic dark chocolate, several slices of homemade banana bread, a small jar of honey, and a free pudding thrown in by the Amish woman. I splurged on a package of mixed squash and carrots—something the kids will never dream of touching, but perfect for stir-fry. Of course, I added a fresh pineapple and a mango to the bag. Then, a long loaf of bread from the Panaderia—the bakery next door.

On the return trip, we stopped in at a small tienda with baby clothes hanging outside. I ended up purchasing two little newborn outfits. The first was slated for Alex's baby doll; the other, a newborn gift for Colocha and Mauricio's new grandson. A corner store yielded a small sheet of wrapping paper and tape—wow, what a find! We were loaded down, and the walk from the bus stop to the house with bulging bolsas was not a fun one. I was silently thankful we had passed on the dozen ears of corn.

Walking is good for you... Only not after dark on a five kilometer stretch of roadway with no streetlights and nothing but animal sounds everywhere...We had been told about the Annual Festival at a local private school down in Playa Chiquita. It turned out to be quite an event. Little girls ran around in bare feet, wearing flowing one-piece gowns; and the adult garb was reminiscent of the flower children of the 1970's. The musical program was comprised of a group of young men and women who sat on the school steps swaying to the beat of bongo drums and tambourines.

As the evening drew to an end, and the group prepared to ignite a massive teepee-looking structure in the center of the 'compound,' we decided it was time to begin walking back toward town. Once again, with hopes of catching a bus midway. We soon ended up in a taxi that took us as far as Charlie's Place for dinner. Afterwards, we hoofed it again for another ten or fifteen minutes until we managed to flag down what looked like a public bus coming our way. As the bus pulled over, we could clearly see the peace signs painted along the sides of the vehicle. We immediately realized *this was not the public bus* but rather, some of the people from the festival we had just left. The young woman with flowing beaded hair was friendly enough though, and we were greeted with smiles all around. A flash of being whisked off into a life of communal living quickly passed and we hopped aboard.

It's not every day we have the opportunity to hitch a ride on a hippie-mobile. We whizzed down the road toward Puerto with tambourines shaking and hands clapping—until the bus got struck between two cars as it tried to maneuver the crowded main street on a Saturday night. The experience was weird enough to even make the kids a bit uneasy; and they were quick to jump up and suggest we take the opportunity to make our getaway before the bus was able to squeeze it's way through the traffic jam.

Downtown Puerto Viejo now has a familiar feel to us. It was good to be back in town. *Our town.* I've decided to approach things from a different perspective from this point on. No more worrying about tomorrow. We're going to enjoy each day as it comes, and experience as much as we possibly can. Earlier in the day, I was speaking with a lady from New York who is here with her 13-year old daughter. I realized just how isolated we've been these past three weeks. We've been so intent on moving in *and fitting in* that we've neglected to do any of the highly publicized 'fun' activities that Puerto Viejo is famous for—like snorkeling, or visiting the iguana farm, or the butterfly reserve. Next week we will begin to explore...

Chapter 12.
Rainy Days and Lessons from Above

June 28th

Here comes the rain... Ah, the fresh smell of damp earth that accompanies the falling rains. I could feel it as we arose early this morning...With a smile I opened the door to the sleeping room knowing I would be greeted by cloudy skies. The rumble of distant thunder blends with the crashing waves, bringing to our ears a soothing melody. When the rains come, they come in slowly. We watch them creeping toward us, dark patches where the already falling sheets move across the land.

The rains are here now, all around us. We're centered, seemingly the only creatures in the universe not in motion. The rain moves as if it is alive. Increasing and decreasing in intensity. Not in sheets, but the slow rain that promises to last for hours. The birds are still moving amidst the trees, although the heavier the rain, the quieter they become.

It's amazing how cool it becomes when the sun is not shining. This morning is reminiscent of the brisk mornings spent on the porch swing in North Carolina. So unlike the steamy Florida rains that rise from the earth and bring a sweat to the brow. There is no putrid acidic smell here when the droplets hit the ground, only the lovely scent of nature.

The rains miraculously bring camaraderie to the children's relationship. They move from project to project with a studied intensity. At the moment it is the inspection of the fifty or so matchbox cars that line the porch from Douglas's play time with Alejandro yesterday. They ponder the dates on the cars, and inquire whether the older ones may be some day worth something.

Nanci brought Alejandro over with her yesterday afternoon...and then left him here. Not the sort of thing a mother in the States would allow—a neighbor taking your child to the home of someone who has been here in the country only three weeks. Really, to the home of a perfect stranger. But perceptions here are different. There is none of the paranoia of child abductions and molestations, of murders and disappearances. Everyone is family, from the moment they arrive, or perhaps from the moment they make it known they are here to stay and not just passing through. Attitudes change noticeably once you are a local. Even the price of commodities and services are occasionally adjusted for those who choose to make their home in this neck of the woods.

Alejandro seemed at ease here in our Caribbean home. Perhaps because the rustic furnishings are somewhat in keeping with the indigenous dwelling he is accustomed to. Our arrival into this new life was a sudden one, moving directly into an open-style home rather than transitioning slowly from our old life to this new one. But now, we find it hard to imagine moving from this place we have come to love, although inevitably the time will come when we may have to move on out of financial necessity.

Equal rights for all... It seems the indigenous people here sometimes do not hold the belief that they are entitled to equal rights. Basic rights, such as the right not to be harassed, the right to file a police report, and the right to utilize public services otherwise available to the citizens of this country. I have begun to observe a sort of hierarchy, with the indigenous seemingly seated squarely at the bottom.

The other day, a boy attacked eleven-year old Carmelita as she passed his house on the way up the hill into the Rainforest. He tore her blouse in half, and Alejandro had to fight him off before he did more harm than we care to fathom. The parents accepted this incident simply as something that happens, something that cannot be helped, that cannot be changed. They were hesitant to seek assistance from the local police ·force and agreed to do so only after Barry pressed the issue with them. The BriBri are such a mild-mannered people, they will wait for hours in a line at the clinic or the bank, only to be told they were in the *wrong* line. Then they simply move to the next line with no complaints.

It seems the personalities of these quiet individuals are formed as they live their secluded existence within the confines of the Rainforest reserves. Even today, technology is considered 'taboo' and the opportunity for the children to play educational computer games at El Puente is a rare one. Alejandro, who is just ten, has had his eyes opened to the expanse of the rest of the world. Whether this is for the better or not is a question yet to be considered. Is it possible to keep the age-old traditions alive while still providing opportunities for the advancement of a people, that they may have a better quality of life? I have a feeling the integration and acceptance of the indigenous is something that will never quite be complete but perhaps it is possible for us to help this process along in small ways, one day at a time...one person at a time.

June 29th

Cleaning Day... Great day! The cleaning lady came this morning—a lovely local woman who happily held a conversation with me in Spanish over a steaming cup of coffee. I don't think it mattered to her that I only understood 50% of what was said. Or maybe I made a good show of it.

She started in the upstairs sleeping rooms and worked her way down. Sweeping, sweeping, sweeping...clomping the broom...sweeping some more. We never knew there was so much dirt under the beds until it began to filter through the floorboards to the bottom level. I've been sweeping every day but apparently not as thoroughly as is necessary. It will be interesting to see how long it takes her to complete this tedious process. Once the upstairs is completed, everything below must be shaken out and wiped down. It will be good to have the floors mopped. She'll use a microbiological agent that supposedly kills all the dangerous microorganisms and neutralizes odor. I'm told it is a natural product that smells like fermented vinegar to the untrained nose.

The cleaning lady tells me she has six children. Four grown children, four grandchildren, and two children still at home—ages seven and nine. She was just released from the hospital last week, after spending eight days attached to an I.V. due to dehydration following a bout with 'la gripe'—the flu. Even now, her arms and left hand still show the telltale signs of being pumped with intravenous fluids. But today she is smiling once again, and glad to be back at work.

The Bull Run... The large white bull was running down the back perimeter fence line, just outside of the yard. We watched it with a bit of humor; then I spotted the girls. Alex and her new friend, Shannen, had just gone outside the fence to free a crab that had the unfortunate luck of spending the afternoon in a tin pot. The neighbor's dog cornered the bull and up it went on its hind legs, breaking through another barbed wire fence directly behind it, and giving it access to the main gravel road. The bull then heard the crab clacking away inside the tin pot, and apparently thought Alex was bringing it dinner. She let out a blood-curdling scream as it lowered its horns and went running straight for her. Luckily, the girls managed to stay out from under it's thundering hooves, although they did return a bit shaken. The bull went running on down the road. Alex can now say with all honesty that she has been in a real bull run! Thank you, St. Christopher...

The Littlest Fisherman... This was the day Douglas had waited for since we first arrived in this fishing paradise. And he skunked them all. He returned from the fishing trip to the old rusty barge downtown with the best catch of any of the men. One needlefish and three beautiful angelfish filled his bucket. In the end, he opted to free the lot of them. The sun set on the horizon as he stood with a wistful look, watching the fish zip away through the breaking waves.

The Deluge... It started as we walked back from Puerto where we'd gone out for pizza this evening. The lights went out in the restaurant just as our meal arrived; and we ended up paying by candlelight. The lack of electricity normally throws everything off in the States, but not so here. Meals at the local café's are frequently prepared on huge outdoor barbeque grills, and bags of candles are kept for just such an occasion. The cash is frequently kept in a tin box behind the counter.

It was sprinkling up until we hit the first tin-roof bus shelter. We stopped for a moment, then decided to keep going. The rain was coming a little harder by the time we reached the shelter nearest the house. It was either make a run for it, or stay there all night. So we ran, with pizza box over our heads. Soon the pizza box made no difference. We stopped running and just walked in the rain.

Alex slipped and got a skinned knee...The first aid kit came out, everybody was wrapped in towels, and we brewed a pot of nice green tea. Ah, home sweet home. As we rushed to close the upstairs shutters, I noticed the usual spot in the kid's room was dripping from the arched ceiling high above. Luckily, the leak is centered between the two beds and doesn't do much harm. We lit the hurricane lamp in anticipation of another power outage, but it never came. So we continued to hang out here in the darkened house—just because.

June 30th

The precious gift of a dove... Sometimes God teaches us lessons in ways that we don't expect. This morning we found a beautiful dove hopping around the side yard. She had an injured wing, probably the result of a hawk that tried to snatch her up in the middle of the night or maybe a possum. Other than the bloodied wing, she seemed fine. Mauricio thought a few days rehabilitation would do the trick so we brought her into the kitchen and made her a nice nest of one of the empty trunks. Heeding his advice, we cooked her some rice and left her a dish of water. She drank from time to time during the day and dozed intermittently. When we arrived home this evening she was still looking chipper and snuggled up as we stroked her head and good wing.

Following our evening movie, Dovey suddenly and unexpectedly passed away. We were all quite upset and couldn't understand what had happened. We had taken such good care of her and she seemed to be on the mend. After the initial shock of finding her lying there on her blanket, Alex suddenly stopped crying and said "God wanted to take her to Heaven so she could fly again." *Her wing must have been so badly injured that she would never have flown and this was His way of giving her the freedom she never would have known here on Earth.* What an awesome thing that my eight-year old daughter was able to see God's grace in the situation.

Chapter 13.
Wild Adventures

The Waterfall... Our new friends, Sheelagh and Shannen, from New York, wanted to take a tour to visit a waterfall near BriBri. So we set out this morning to do the 'tourist' thing and accompany them on their hike. The tour was led by a young Brit and his long-haired Americano cohort. Two ancient VW buses were parked in front of their business, which doubles (or triples) as a sidewalk café and Laundromat.

The tour started out with a rather humbling walk single-file down the main street with several other tourists, to none other than—the public bus stop. We boarded the bus in a herd and waited patiently as it slowly made it's way past the turnoff to our house and toward BriBri. The bus turned off in familiar territory, near la clinica at Hone Creek, and then proceeded up the mountain pass. The first leg of the journey ended just before the landslides, where we disembarked and continued on foot. I nervously glanced at the raw dirt trickling slowly from the mountainside looming off to the right. It appeared much more ominous from our vantage point as pedestrians.

After crossing the bridge, we passed through a wooden

gate to the left and started out down the muddy path. It was now sprinkling rain but too difficult to keep our footing while holding onto an umbrella. The 'guides'—and I will use that word cautiously—were far ahead, not giving much thought to the group of nine women and children following them. There was no explanation of flora, nor fauna, nor wildlife. Just trying to keep up with the guides. Finally, we reached the bottom of the hill near the rushing headwaters, where each one of us was treated to a climb up the hillside clinging to a thick nylon rope. Douglas, who had stayed 500 feet ahead of us for the entire hike, nimbly scaled the hill, up and then down again, right alongside the guides.

It was pouring rain once we reached the waterfall, so we all decided to take a swim in the pool at the foot of the *cascada grande*. What the heck, we were already soaked. It was a spectacular waterfall, the rushing water so powerful it was impossible to muster enough strength to pull oneself up underneath the cascades. The kids chilled quickly and were soon sitting under the circle of umbrellas shielding our bags and cameras. The group of girls from London started to look a little glum as they huddled together in the freezing water; and a unanimous vote was soon taken to head back to the bus stop, although our allotted hour was not yet up.

Scaling the side of the cliff after the rain had fallen was a bit more daunting. The kids made it up the hill and down the rope, but poor Jungle Mom went swinging out over the riverbed, nearly cutting the second guide in half with the blue nylon rope. Once at the bottom of the riverbed, we all trudged on ahead up the slippery mountain, ninety percent of us barefoot, as the guides assisted the last two stragglers with the rope decent.

Since we were off schedule, the entire group rushed down the highway trying in vain to catch the next bus into town. We missed the bus, and watched as pathetic dripping blobs as it sped past. With no need to hurry now, everyone stopped to take a rest at the nearest tin overhang, amusing ourselves as we watched some locals unload cartons of *manzanas de agua*—water apples.

Douglas, sensing our discouragement, tried his best to cheer everyone up. First, he picked a flower for Shannen… then one for me…then one for Alex…then, what the heck, one for Shannen's mom and then one for each of the five girls from London. The guides felt left out, so he soon came back with red flowers for them as well. Seeing that we were hungry and miserable, Douglas characteristically began to scrounge up the manzanas that were being thrown into the grass—the smaller ones, not quite ripe, but still edible, that were being discarded by the Ticos at the roadside stand.

The great thing is that you will never starve in a Rainforest. Nanci and I mused the other day that even if the roads to San Jose were to be blocked for an entire month, we would still manage to survive in our little corner of the world for the food all around us.

A temporary lull in the steady rainfall and we headed further down the mountain to the actual bus stop. There we all took some nice photos of the mountains as the afternoon mist rose above them. We spotted a pig at the farm across the road—bets were he was 700 pounds or more. The bus finally arrived and we were oblivious to the darting looks we received as we boarded. I'm sure the bus driver was none too happy to see us dragging our muddy, wet selves onto his spotless bus.

July 2nd

Gravelly Gravel…Yesterday we woke up to find the road had been re-graveled all the way from Playa Negra to Puerto Viejo. This apparently happens from time to time and is something that must be tolerated. It should have been a good thing, because the two-day rains had washed away much of the existing roadway, leaving large pits and puddles to maneuver around. But the road is rough going by bicycle even on a good day. We did our best to avoid being sucked into the ditch time after time until we finally made it to the smooth patch at the entrance to town. Walking to town was not any easier; we actually broke our own rules and took the bus twice in the same day.

Coming back from town this evening, the dust was particularly thick. At one point, we were surrounded by so much of the stuff that Douglas—with outstretched arms and eyes clamped tightly shut yelled—"Mommy, where are you...I can't find you!" Said with a bit of humor, but not really much of a stretch of the imagination. The cars were coming at us with their lights on, although it was only 3 pm. I guess gravel makes dust...?

Chapter 14.
Reflections on a Month Well-Spent

It's our anniversary! The month has been well spent and we've begun the transition from our 'honeymoon' in Costa Rica to living here full-time. Every day holds new experiences. There have been a few frustrations, but also as many wondrous discoveries and rewarding moments. We wake up refreshed, the kids climb into my bed smiling, the birds singing...The days are longer here and we have more time together than we've ever had.

We've had difficulty getting into the home school routine. The kids fight it when I bring out the books and we've yet to see more than one short activity sheet completed daily. I'm not worried too much about this because things will change soon and the kids will need to be enrolled in school. The job is right around the corner and I'm looking forward to feeling useful once again.

There is a world of nature still to explore, the world of the indigenous culture, the world of the Caribbean lifestyle. My children are not suffering for the experience, they are learning, they are growing and they will continue to grow. Nothing worth doing is ever easy—but I didn't expect this to be easy. Some days, I'm ready to pack it in and come back to the States. Some days I cannot imagine ever living in the States again. I have to remind myself from time to time why I really moved here—for the simplicity of life, the camaraderie of a small community, for the eclectic mix of cultures and ideas. It's hard to put into words the feel of really *being here* but it's like nothing I've ever experienced. I miss my friends, my family, but I also feel that somehow this move has brought us closer. There is a purpose in everything. A coworker said to me before I left that he thought I was searching for something, but that it was not something I would find in a faraway country, rather something I was searching for *within myself.* Perhaps that is true. But the journey toward self-discovery has to begin somewhere. Without the confines of an eight to five job I find my mind beginning to open up and some days I'm able to regain the creativity of youth. I hope to continue this journey because to stop learning is to stop living. And living in the real sense of the word is not to simply exist behind concrete walls. It's experiencing each day to the fullest. I'll quote one of Barry's old newsletters in which he said that when you wake up here you face everything head on—*the good, the bad and the ugly.* Life here is not always pretty but it's real, not the watered-down version. I believe that's part of what I was searching for.

Things I Miss About the United States

- Family. Seeing my sister and her children. Sitting in the living room of my parent's house. Visiting with grandma. My son and daughter-in-law.
- Food. Eating out. Making good meals. Having an oven. Pop N' Fresh Rolls, ready to bake Pillsbury cookies. Shopping for groceries all in one place. Having a car to put the groceries into.
- Friends. Having lunch together. Emails back and forth. Conversations. Having a companion to go out to dinner with, movies on the big screen—with air conditioning, popcorn and sodas—and no insects. Drinks out.

- Air conditioning. Not in the early morning or evenings, but between 10 and 4, the longest and hottest part of the day.
- My Montero, the best vehicle I ever owned.
- Having my own house. Having more space for the kids to spread out. Having a room to go to and a door I can shut.
- Theme parks.

Things I Value About Costa Rica

- Always hearing the ocean.
- The birds and butterflies that fly through the living room.
- The excitement of a horned beetle buzzing unexpectedly into the kitchen, or a bat that's gotten into the upstairs bedroom and can't get out.
- The hummingbirds—all day long, flitting from tree to tree, flower to flower. Their vivid colors.
- The parrots we see downtown perched on the buildings. The parrots you can play with at Hot Rocks, a local outdoor café.
- The long walks into Puerto with the beach always visible. The walk back from town along the beach itself as the sun sets on the horizon.
- The bus ride into Limon. Watching the people. Shopping at Mas X Menos and reveling in the American products we find there.
- The newness of the culture, learning to adapt, finding alternate ways of doing things.
- The rapport I've built through email with friends and family, even out-of-state family that I haven't corresponded with in years.
- The new friends I've made. The way people here become so close so fast. The camaraderie.
- The feeling of not always being comfortable. Not always being at the ideal temperature. Getting caught in a downpour. Learning to accept what comes each day.

Chapter 15.
The Serenity of Self

July 3rd

A rare day...sin niños! The children's dad arrived first thing this morning, as promised, and whisked them away for a day of fishing and swimming. Alex wanted to stay with me, as she had last Sunday, but I needed a day. *Let's just call it a mental health day.*

It's amazing how much more I'm able to observe and process without the chattering of children all around. It's a welcome respite, and I've come to look forward to these occasional days alone.

I'm considering a bicycle ride along the beach, or maybe a bus ride to Manzanillo, to explore and have lunch at the great seafood restaurant called Maxi's. Much has been accomplished already—the dishes, the sweeping. The beds are made, and the laundry is hanging, freshly washed, from the bright green porch railings.

Yesterday was a great clean-out day. When I made the mistake of mentioning to the kids that if things don't work out here for the long-term, maybe we'd go back to the States—they spent the next two hours rummaging through their things, repacking their trunks, and discarding some of the toys and books they had brought with them. We now have about four grocery bags full—shoes that are no longer serviceable, storybooks, coloring books, and toys—that will soon be donated to The Bridge. With the impending move across the fence to the smaller house mid-August, I was secretly glad the kids had repacked their toys rather than having them scattered everywhere throughout the house. It will make things easier when the time comes. Part of the agreement when we moved in was to relocate for those thirteen days in August—due to a previous rental commitment. An inconvenience, certainly, but it's not the end of the world.

A walk through the mountains... Rather than heading south, I opted to go into BriBri in search of a few items that I haven't been able to find in town—ice cube trays, hair color—things we've been doing without—*important things*. I ended up walking from the house to Hone Creek—about 5 kms—and then catching the bus from there. The trip was a success, although the town appeared a bit sleepy this Sunday afternoon. There were a few stores open—the main grocery, the bakery, another smaller grocery across the street and a small tienda with a little bit of everything along one of the secluded side roads. The stores here are reminiscent of the typical General Store featured in all the old Westerns, and can be likened perhaps to Ike Godsey's business on the television series 'The Waltons'. Everything is stacked up neatly, with shirts and pants piled high, shoes hanging on the walls, and the back wall typically lined with building supplies and sundries.

My favorite roperia/zapateria—clothing and shoe store— was open when I arrive in town, although they closed down at noon, as many businesses typically do. I wandered into the open-air café next to the grocery store and ran into Sue, the Americana writer, and Anita, a timeless BriBri woman who has a wonderful sense of humor, coupled with a strong character. It was good to see familiar faces among the dozens of strangers I had passed throughout the day. Lunch consisted of a typical 'casado' with moist, homemade cornbread for dessert.

After spending as much time as I possibly could on the only street in town, I sat down and waited for the next bus. This is something I soon tire of, so I chose the obvious route and started out down the mountain on foot. Surely a bus will come along at some point. Worse case scenario—Puerto Viejo is only 10 kilometers away—*or is it 13 kilometers as the next sign says?* Surely one of them must be correct.

The walk through the mountains was one of the most beautiful I've ever taken. Surprisingly, it wasn't all-downhill, rather little ups and downs along the way. Off to the right was a B*uena Vista*—a beautiful view of the valley with the Talamanca mountain range towering above. Small wooden one-room houses peeked out here and there from among the dense vegetation. Walking is really the only way to go. It's impossible to see and feel everything about a place while passing through in a car or bus, even at 35 mph. The familiar sounds were all around—in stereo—the birds, the bugs—I call them the jungle sounds. At one point, I heard the distant beat of drums, which conjured up images of the indigenous dwellings from which these sounds must have emanated.

About half way through the mountain pass, I met a family waiting at a bus shelter and inquired whether a bus would pass by there soon. They were expecting one at 1:30 pm, so I stood and waited with them for nearly an hour. A discussion, in Spanish, ensued, and the husband, wife and six children speculated as to where the bus was and whether they should start walking toward Hone Creek to pick up the pills prescribed yesterday for the father. The middle boy of about ten sat across the road by himself. A teenage daughter held the baby, and a toddler entertained them all by swinging her arms at an older boy as he incessantly teased her. The father entertained himself at a distance with his machete, first cutting and skinning a walking stick, then turning the machete over to the ten-year old. The boy took a few swings before climbing up into a tree high above the bus shelter. His antics were short-lived though, as everyone soon agreed he should stop swinging on the vine or he would surely fall down the steep incline into the riverbed below.

The bus never came; I said goodbye to the family and continued my trek toward town. Since no one was expecting to see an Americana walking down the mountain, I understandably drew a few curious looks as I passed each house along the way. At one point, the need for agua almost got me, but I managed to survive most of the way on the last of the warm Coca-Cola purchased with my lunch.

Near the intersection at Hone Creek I was finally able to flag a bus. I sunk down into the cushioned seat and rode the last 3 kilometers into town. Technically, I had walked the entire distance to BriBri—from the casita to Hone Creek, and then from BriBri back to Hone Creek. Nanci commended me later, stating this was surely another notch to be added to my belt.

Chapter 16.
Lazy, Crazy Days

July 5th

The 4th of July was a bust…The shipment of fireworks that was supposed to have arrived at Hot Rocks never made it, so we watched the first of two movies on the big screen and then made our way home via taxista. I think they see us coming now, as a group of two or three will inevitably start yelling "Taxi? Taxi?" as we pass by. Some days I turn them down, but not very often after dark. 1,000 colones isn't much to ask to avoid that dark stretch of roadway, especially now with the choking dust still rising from the main road. It's hard to fathom why it hasn't rained here for nearly a week when we're living in the middle of a tropical rainforest. When it rains, it pours, but the cool respite from the heat of the day is short-lived. A morning rain is gone by noon, and a nighttime rain, by morning. The plants along the roadway have adopted a permanent brown caramel color and the chairs in every café must be dusted off before one considers sitting down.

The long afternoon spent at home is coming to an end, and the cool breezes are starting to filter through the house. The best place to sit is on the steps between the first and second level where a cross-breeze seems to always be found. Douglas is still napping in the hammock. He had a bout with an itchy eye this morning and the antihistamine administered as a safety measure seems to have taken its toll. No matter, we were up again part of the night with another 'Mommy, I'm throwing up' scene, so a nap will do us all some good.

Next week will mark a change in our routine. I plan to actively seek a school in which to enroll the children. They made friends with a group of kids down at the beach in front of the police station yesterday. It was amazing to watch the transformation in their personalities as they were engaged in nearly three hours of playtime. We ended up bringing home a gorgeous wiggly sea urchin, luckily of the purple variety. One of the new friends advised us that if the *red sea urchin* stings you five times, you would then DIE. I sure am glad we didn't bring that one home. We also found out that the huge bloated toads sitting underneath the stilts of many of the downtown businesses are capable of spitting poison in the face of their aggressor when they feel threatened.

Vipers in the yard, tarantulas in the house, scorpions in the bathroom, spitting toads, pretty little red poison arrow frogs the size of a fingernail...A friend once said to me that she would rather be bitten by a viper than to die in a fiery crash on the California freeway. I guess everything just needs to be kept in perspective.

July 6th

Gone to the dogs... The dogs here add a certain bit of character to the area. Scrawny stray dogs are all around. All the same shape, some smaller, some larger, they appear to be cut from an identical mold. They're always docile, never vicious, and usually with ribs showing. It's not uncommon to see a woeful face looking up at you while you dine. In fact, it's rather uncommon NOT to see one. They walk the streets freely, seeming to belong to no one, yet in a sense belonging to all or maybe to the town itself.

Today it was a black one that befriended us at dinner. He

positioned himself squarely to my left, knowing instinctively I was the only one with meat on my plate. He had no interest in the kid's pizza, nor in the pile of French fries. I eventually gave in to his unblinking stare, as he knew I would, and tossed him a small piece of chicken. He soon returned and sat patiently waiting for more.

Last week a dog followed us at least three kilometers as we carried a bolsa of leftovers—all the way through town, through the pouring rain, and onto our front porch. The downpour was his saving grace, as he normally would never have made it past the landlord's two German Shepard's and into the gated yard. This particular evening the gate was open and we had run through it trying to avoid the lightning and unrelenting rain. Sometime during the night the storm passed and we heard the pitiful yelps of the poor stray as the Shepard's chased him away. They do add a sense of security to this place although it is sometimes carried to the extreme. The night before last, the on-site dogs were occupied with keeping a wayward horse at bay. Frenzied barking and the thumping that accompanies their escape from underneath our living room floorboards was heard repeatedly throughout the night.

July 7th

Limon is not such a bad place...I met Colin, a Canadian neighbor, on the way to the bus stop this morning and we discussed in length the unfair rap Limon has been given. As long as one does not venture out at night, the port city situated an hour to the north really does have a bit of character. I thought about our conversation on the way in this morning and decided to look at Puerto Limon in a different light.

As the bus turns the corner near the airstrip, the port city becomes visible from a distance, usually surrounded by several freightliners and with a bit of luck, a cruise ship or two. Regardless of whether you are a tourist, an extranjero or a Tico raised here all your life—every head turns toward the port at this point in the journey.

Today the kids and I discovered the extensive downtown marketplace packed with dozens of vendors peddling fruits and vegetables in every imaginable color and texture. We wandered aimlessly down several streets we never knew existed, and managed to gain a better feel for the city. The main drag is always crowded and it's impossible to walk very far without bumping into someone or other. The congestion is thicker around the bus stops and thins out as one walks toward the oceanfront Parque Vargas. Today we stopped at the usual snow cone vendor in the park—the one who sits directly across from City Hall. Remarkably, he remembered us from our last trip to the city and commented, "Sin leche, no?" meaning we would like our shaved ice without milk, right? The shaved ice delicacy sold at the local roadside stands is served not only with the typical sugary syrup topping found on snow cones purchased in the States; it is also topped with a slathering of canned sweetened condensed milk.

Truth or Fiction? We encountered a con-man first jump off the bus, who tried to convince me he was someone I had previously met in Puerto Viejo. He was in Limon visiting his grandmother, who he claimed lay dying of cancer in the hospital. His mother and two sisters had been in town visiting her, and now needed the bus fare to get back to Puerto. He assured me he would pay me back with a combination of colones and a supply of fresh fish and camerones—shrimp—within the next week and asked several times how much interest I would like to charge him.

I couldn't help remembering a passage I had just read not two days ago in my Daily Devotional for Parents. It was a passage about giving to someone who asks, even if you are quite sure they are not legit. It was about giving with a joyful heart and letting God deal with the other person. My children's eyes were upon me and the moral dilemma grew, but then I saw behind the man a newspaper vendor vigorously motioning to me not to do it. Another man in uniform, perhaps a security guard, passed by and with a nod of his head indicated to me this was a scam. I finally made the excuse that if I gave him the 5000 colones for the bus fare, I would not be able to purchase the groceries I had come into town for—the food I needed for my children. I suggested that perhaps there might be someone else he could ask for the money. The con-man made a quick getaway and the kids seemed to accept the outcome. A brief acknowledgment as I passed the newspaper vendor—*fue un mentiroso*—he was a liar—cemented the fact that this man had indeed been a con-artist. I'm wondering if perhaps I made the wrong choice as far a teaching my children to 'give cheerfully' but on the other hand their physical needs—the food purchased with that 5000 colones—is a responsibility that falls to me as well. It's tough to maintain an equal balance.

Oddly enough, another unfamiliar man approached us while we were sitting in the park. This one was named George and also claimed to have known us from Puerto Viejo. He mentioned several times that he'd just recently gotten a haircut, and suggested that was the reason I didn't recognize him. This one was peddling fried meat pies and once the conversation began, he didn't continue to push his wares. Perhaps he really was someone we have seen in passing. In any event, I kept my bag close at hand just to be on the safe side.

We arrived at Limon Central Park at the usual mid-day, so many of the locals were sitting on the park benches relaxing during the two-hour break they receive for lunch. Several vendors dotted the landscape, not doing much business—mostly just chatting with friends. A couple of beatniks tapped on a pair of bongos as they occupied the steps near the oceanfront view of the Isla. A blanket was outstretched in front of them for 'contributions'.

Douglas commented that there was an enchanted deserted island right in front of us. He'd never noticed it there before, sitting just off the shoreline. I vaguely remember the island from a trip to Limon long ago, although the photos I brought back from that trip were taken from a higher vantage point at a national park just north of the city.

I found my coffee—five bags of deep, dark, robust Vanilla Nuez—the flavor I had run out of, and have been desperately craving for the past week. I admit the coffee was the underlying reason for the hour and a half bus ride to and from the port city. Mas X Menos, the major grocery store chain in Limon, has a lot of items that can't be had in our neck of the woods; and it's definitely worth any inconvenience to get there. All in all, our trip to Limon was a great success.

July 8th

The Pleasures of Shopping...I love the ride into BriBri. The turn off at Hone Creek, then the winding road up the mountain—past the landslides, past the waterfall. All is intimately familiar territory now, ever since The Walk. Today we were fortunate to receive an offer to go with Nanci while she picked up the weekly food bolsas. This has become a ritual, riding along with her either on Tuesday to place the order, or on Friday, to pick it up. We never know as we leave the house in the morning where the day will lead us, but we've learned to jump when opportunity presents itself.

The bakery in this small mountain town is by far the best around. A loaf of sweet cheese bread can be had for 380 colones, about 75 cents, and we always have trouble deciding whether to take home a long, crispy loaf of French bread, or a fat loaf of squishy Italian. Today it was the Italian, with a dusting of flour on top—and three fresh chocolate frosted donuts.

Shopping here is *different*. Nothing like strolling down the endless aisles at Wal-Mart. It's all about hunting, searching, and mentally retaining all those little details of what can be found where. And the funny thing about it is that nothing remains constant. There are so many variables that go into the equation. Maybe the weather has caused a road to be blocked to San Jose. Maybe a strike has prevented the delivery trucks from passing for several hours, or several days. Perhaps a landslide has occurred along the slippery mountain road...

One never knows what commodity will suddenly be missing from the shelves on any given day. Take for example—paper towels. An item that in our old lives was pretty much a given. I remember well a friend whose parents purchased the things by the dozens and stored them piled high on the back porch—along with the toilet paper and cases of canned soda pop. Not so here.

Today there were no paper towels to be had in Puerto—none at Buen Precio, none at Jeffrey's. There were none to be had at either store in BriBri. I thought perhaps it was just a little mala suerte on my part—the fact that we had been draining our bacon on the kitchen dish towel for two or three days now. But when Nanci told us she had encountered the same problem, we set out on a common mission.

We finally found the paper towels at a small grocery along the main road, just north of Hone Creek. We had stopped there on a whim, just hoping…it's the little things that bring pleasure here, and a sense of accomplishment.

Chapter 17.
More Lessons Learned

July 10th

Incommunicado... The month of July is fast slipping away. I find myself living in an isolated bubble sometimes and only hear of 'big news' from other extranjeros in the area. Sure, I occasionally glance down at the headlines of 'El Diario' the daily newspaper that sits on the counter at Jeffrey's—but I rarely buy one. And paying a premium price to access my emails at the local Internet café, I no longer have the luxury of reading the on-line news daily. It's nerve-wracking enough to spend 45 minutes on the so-called 'Satellite' Internet to open as few as three or four email messages. Many times when the café is filled, it's impossible to even move past the sign-in screen. I wish to apologize for the brevity of the responses I've been sending back, but there's no other way than to just send a couple lines back to each person who has contacted me. I'm hoping the newsletter, which is prepared here at the house and then downloaded the next morning at the café, has enough substance to keep the lines of communication alive.

Phone communication has also turned out to be nearly

non-existent for us, at least for the time being. We were able to call mom and dad from a friend's house one time when we first arrived but this is not a privilege I wish to overuse. The international phone card I purchased does not, for some unknown reason, allow calls to the U.S., although it will allow us to call anywhere else in the world...We're hoping to someday have our own phone line and internet at the house but I've been waiting to get into a more permanent place before we tackle the red tape that's involved in that process.

Eaten alive... There's no way to get around it. Living in the open, we get bit. We get bit by all kinds of insects that we never actually see. We get bit *continually*. Day, night, evening. Downtown. At home. During soup kitchen. During movie night. We use insect repellant. We wear long pants when we go to the outdoor movie theatre. We use mosquito nets when we sleep at night.

We love living in this house, it's like being a part of nature. We sit here in the open living room and we feel as if we are in the rainforest. Birds swoop in and out, butterflies flutter through. The lizard that stands up and runs on it's hind legs across the yard jumps from tree to tree right in front of our eyes. And the geckos...well, we commune with the geckos. They run in and out of the walls. The kids chase them from the bedrooms to the downstairs, to the outside of the house and back again...it's a nightly ritual. So we are torn between the two choices—to move to a house with screens and bars on the windows, or to remain in this open house and continue to live with the insect problem.

One day when we arrived home after a steady rain, the crazy ants had invaded the bathroom. They were coming in through the cracks in the cement, and when I sprayed the only thing I had on hand, insect repellant, of course, they poured out of the shower, covering it like a moving black blanket. Each ant carried a little white egg and I was told later that this is a ritual they perform when they feel a big storm coming—they must carry their eggs to safety.

July 11th

Mangoes, mangoes…After soup kitchen on Saturday, Daniel (pronounced more like don-yell) announced he was taking the kids to a nearby farm to pick mangoes. So my two little tenderfoots trekked off in flip-flops to the mango farm. Two hours later, I was a little concerned. Daniel is very trustworthy, I've been told. He raised his family years ago and spends his time now working at El Puente and watching out for the neighborhood kids. He is rarely found without an entourage. One can always spot him across the street from the Stevens as the bus pulls up after school, buying (and eating) ice cream with the children. He speaks fluent BriBri and Spanish and I'm told he really does speak English as well, although he refuses to do so with me. He did the same thing to Barry for the first year, and we have a theory that this is more or less 'for our own good.'

Daniel with friends Catie, Maria, William and Carmelita

Nanci finally convinced me to go on home and take advantage of the time alone. She would bring the kids along later. They arrived not five minutes after I stepped out of the shower, toting bags of mangoes, none larger than a baseball—

but better than any I've ever had from the market. Both were very muddy and terribly tired, but they seemed to have enjoyed themselves. When asked to describe the experience, my children told me of a hike through the forest until they came to a clearing where the mango trees were interspersed among other rainforest vegetation. Many of the mangoes had just fallen and were easily picked up off the ground. Hence the reason Daniel had been so eager to go out to the farm today. It seems the large variety of fruits here come and go in three or four predictable cycles throughout the year. *Mangoes anyone?*

Responsibility... If nothing else, Douglas has been learning the meaning of responsibility. He's formed a new daily routine, jumping on his bicycle as I turn on the kettle for the morning coffee, and returning ten minutes later with four freshly baked rolls from Jeffrey's in his backpack. He carefully counts out 600 colones, sometimes bringing more with him just in case he hits the jackpot and finds a package of bacon as well. He always returns with a smile on his face, unable to mask the pride in this new accomplishment. There's something to be said of living in a small town. I can't imagine ever having sent him off to the corner Kwik King for morning rolls...

The new hammock... We finally broke down and bought a new hammock. The old frayed hammock that was here when we moved in has disintegrated to the point of no longer being safe. The new one is colorful, made of macramé string woven together in an intricate pattern, and sports a large wooden stick at either end. The only problem is, when the kids start playing around with this newer version, the sticks start hitting everything—the wall, the other furniture, heads, various body parts. I'm not sure how long the hammock will last before I'll have to take it down, but it sure is pretty!

July 12th

We've Got Mail! Today was a good day. First of all, we got a haircut. Well, two of us got a haircut. Alex is in the process of growing out her bangs—again. The man who cut our hair asked my daughter when she was going to come back in to see him. I told him he'd be waiting a long time. She's actually only had her hair professionally twice—in nearly nine years.

I met Randy in March when he was moving into the apartment next to Joyce /aka/ The Juice Queen. He apparently was a barber or hairstylist of some sort in his previous life, because the haircuts he gave us for about the equivalent of $4 were better than we've had in years. A peek inside his apartment revealed a bit of creativity. The front glass had been replaced by screening, letting in a cool breeze, and a *real gas stove* (versus the stove TOP that the rest of us have) sat in the center of a kitchen island crafted from bamboo poles found along the beach. I'm told he bakes as well...

The second unexpected event of the day was the arrival of 'the package,' a large box tied onto the back of the local Correo motorbike. The Correo or post office employee drove right up to the front door of the house, asking for my signature and the ever-important passport number.

I was left with a large box that had been sent by my parents, and surrounded by two little jumping, squealing children. They tore open the box even before I could locate the scissors and Alex unashamedly also tore open her birthday gift—slated for August 11th, nearly a month away. It was Christmas all over again. The box contained numerous packages of Jello chocolate pudding mix, the legendary Lipton noodle 'Grandma' soup packets, dish towels, tank tops (a Godsend), sand toys, a potato masher (no more mashing with a fork), and a Popsicle maker. All items were immensely appreciated.

Craft supplies overflowed—construction paper, markers, coloring books, and watercolors. The kids were finally *occupied* and I realized that what we've been fighting has been boredom brought on by a lack of constructive activities. Alex made me sit for nearly 30 minutes while she drew a portrait that now hangs on my bedroom wall. Then she made a Thank You card with her new markers for Nonnie and PopPop. We feel loved.

July 13th

No! Don't throw that away... One of the lessons we're learning here is the value of thriftiness. Materialism is no longer a part of our lives. And we are learning that when you live in a place where things are hard to come by, everything is considered valuable. There is very little waste, very few throw-aways. The piece of twine that held together the new hammock, the elastic band that came on the bag of bread... things like that are kept just in case they're needed later on down the road. Ziploc baggies are rinsed out and reused. I even found myself reusing a piece of *tin foil* that had come home with some leftovers one night.

Someone sent a large box of toys to El Puente—the kind of toys that you find in the bottom of a toy box. The kids spent an afternoon going through those little pieces and parts, trying to sort and make sense of piles of old Barbies without dresses, little plastic figurines that come in McDonald's happy meals, stray Legos—sorting and trying to make sense of things that in our old lives were simply dumped into a big green garbage bag once every six months—and discarded. It was an eye-opening experience. My children were able to see first-hand the fascination that held the BriBri children as they made their way through the colorful pile of 'stuff'.

It seems the longer we are here, the less interested my children are in the few toys they brought with them. They've given away many things that they were unable to part with only a month ago when we moved, and don't seem to miss them at all. For the most part, the toys they still have stay in the trunks, unused. They play outdoors, they play on the beach, we ride bikes, and they color and paint. Their old stuffed animal collection has become an integral part of the imaginary play that takes place in our household now. Without as much clutter, the children are able to conjure up games and activities simply out of their imaginations. They catch butterflies and insects, guppies and crawfish. The kitchen pots and colanders are always in use.

Joyce and I talked about how we miss yard sales and thrift stores. How it was such a waste of time, energy and money, to purchase new clothes at the retail stores, only to watch those items fall apart within weeks. How higher quality clothing could be had at thrift stores, and Goodwill stores. Take for example, the shirt that I for the most part live in now—a green button-up sleeveless blouse—purchased for less than $1 at a thrift store in North Carolina just before the move. And in contrast, the stack of new t-shirts purchased from a department store, already stretched out and faded, that have since been given away.

I'll never look at things in quite the same way again, even if we are to return to the States one day. There will be no more charging more than we actually earn, no more wasting precious resources. There will be more of a conscious effort to comply with the recycling programs, more of a conscious effort to purchase only those things we need—rather than want. I look at the way the houses are built here, the way people accept what they have, and live for the most part very happily and content with so little.

I recall driving down one of the main drags in our hometown, where wooden shacks line the roadway, and feeling bad, feeling sorry for those people. But I realize now that perhaps they had something that those of us who lived in the concrete-block houses didn't. In that apparent 'bad' neighborhood, we also observed an unfamiliar phenomenon. Everywhere we looked, there were always people walking, riding bicycles, and talking on their front porches with the neighbors. In the end, that's what is really important. It's not the things we have, but the lives that we touch.

Chapter 18.
Summer Rains, Breezy Nights

July 14th

The Third Rain...last night was the third *cool night* and the arrival of dawn marked the end of the third rain. And that means no more dust on the gravel road. The constant stream of traffic has now successfully pounded in the larger of the rocks, and the rain has helped to meld the roadway into one solid surface.

We're ecstatic about the nights, which have been so cool for most of this week that we've pulled all of our blankets out of the trunks and turned off the fans. It was unexpected, this cool spell, and thus that much more appreciated. The mosquitoes seem to have sensed this change in the weather and despite the rain, have dwindled in numbers—at least for the time being. The funny thing is, for all the insect bites, I have yet to actually *see* a mosquito.

A neighbor told me the other day that the dengue-carrying breed is a day-biter and can be distinguished by the bright white tip at the end of its stinger. I'm always more leery when an itchy bump starts to rise during the day because dengue is one disease for which preventative measures cannot be taken. There really is no cure, save for symptomatic relief.

Limon, again... When we took our weekly bus trip to Limon yesterday, a carnival with small kiddie rides was setting up near the park. Much to the children's disappointment, the process had not yet been completed and I have no way of knowing when the carnival will actually be in full swing. The trip included our usual stroll downtown to Parque Vargas and this time led to the discovery of a rock climbing wall at the water's edge—next to the pile of rubble left from the quake of 1991 that ripped through this small port town. It was a 7.5 on the Richter scale if I recall correctly.

I had the foresight this trip to bring my camera and got some great shots of the park, the enchanted deserted island, and the quake damage. My photos are not always pretty, but they invariable tell a story. Maybe I was a journalist in a previous life or perhaps that is what I aspire to be.

Goodbye Don Pablo... It seems the local police force in Puerto occasionally takes things into its own hands. Maybe it's simpler that way. Definitely cheaper than the long drawn out judicial process that must be endured in the States. Don Pablo, the Fence, is gone. Burned to the ground. In place of his house /aka/ Pawn Shop where he marketed various stolen goods—sits a guard, a local policeman with an AK-47. Twenty-four hours a day, even on Sundays. Tired of the constant citizen complaints, rumor has it that La Policia did what was necessary to end a nagging problem. There is something to be said for simple justice.

Healthier living... One of the many reasons for the move to Costa Rica was to make a drastic lifestyle change, something that try as I might, I never could seem to do in the States. Two or three years ago I suddenly and unexpectedly gained over twenty pounds in a very short period of time. There are many theories for this dilemma. Perhaps the added weight could be attributed to a new medication I was taking, maybe it was hormonal changes brought on by my approach toward the big 4-0. Who really knows what caused my body to do this strange and unwelcome thing?

I'm happy to report that the transformation I had hoped for has begun to occur. Maybe due to the miles and miles a day that we walk, maybe due to bicycles being our only mode of transportation. Less stress? Healthier foods? In any event, the body that six weeks ago barely squeezed into size 12 clothing now fits comfortably in the size 10 jeans brought with us only on a whim. The Larges are too large and the only complaint I have is that I have no clothes left that actually fit...*God is good.*

July 15th

The warmth of a spring morning... Or is it a summer morning, or a winter morning? We never really know what 'season' it is from old standards—only that we are supposedly in the 'green' versus the 'dry' season right now. I know this because hotel prices are down. Last night was once again cool, but as soon as the sun hit the living room—around 7 am—we could tell today was going to be a hot one. It's funny how we delight in the rain and fresh breezes one day, yet we also welcome the sunny days as this means the laundry lining the porch will actually dry, and can finally be put away.

Hanging laundry seems to be a part of the décor around here, accepted as a set of new curtains would be accepted in the States. It's a part of daily life. The Rastafarians and Ticos alike appear to live the same happy existence—somewhat separate yet subtly intertwined in their lives. *Everyone's porches are lined with laundry.*

The face of desperation... We stopped at the home of an indigenous woman on the way back from BriBri today—to purchase a new bunch of bananas to be hung on the porch to ripen. This family lives in a small wooden shack and sells the large bunches of unripe bananas for 500 colones each. The shack is precariously perched atop a hill and you can see the dirty wooden floor through the haphazardly placed sheets of tin and plywood that serve as four walls. I fear that with the history of landslides in the area, one day we will arrive to find their home crumpled in a heap in the valley below.

The mother appeared to be away this day, and a young girl reluctantly came out to greet us. She expectedly wore tattered, soiled clothing, but it was her expression that captured my attention. This girl could have been no more than twelve, but she had the defeated look of an 80-year old. A look that held no hope, a small face incapable of seeing even beyond today. Her future is bleak, I am sure, and I harbored no hard feelings when she failed to return with the change for my purchase. Nanci disagreed with my statement that surely this family could use the 500 colones—a dollar—more than I needed it. She said they are notorious for conning people, pulling a fast one, and to let it go would be to further encourage the unacceptable behavior. How sad that a child must grow up learning such lessons, never really having the chance to decipher right from wrong but doing what she must so that she and her younger siblings will have bread to eat tonight.

I am beginning to better understand the circumstances from which the people at Saturday Soup Kitchen come. Why they walk from as far as Hone Creek for a simple bowl of vegetable soup and crackers. I cannot imagine living in such dire poverty yet I know in my heart it was only the luck of the draw that I was born where and when I had been born. *So easily, this could be me.* I couldn't help but see the face of my own tiny daughter reflected in the indigenous child's eyes today. I'm so grateful for the opportunities I've been given, the education I've received, but most of all, I'm grateful for the chance to become a part of something that has the potential to make a difference in these precious lives.

There is potential here. We can see vividly the new buildings, the shower facilities, and the playroom and craft area for the children. The Stevens have come so far, breaking through barriers that had been up for decades, but there is much more to be done. Nanci tells me of the way it was the first few months she served soup. None of the women smiled. They came, they ate, and they left quietly. There was no joy, no communion. Now the women laugh and joke, they share in the entertainment after the meal, and they confide in Nanci.

El Puente has become a gathering place for families who reside in different geographic areas—the opportunity for children and grandmothers to visit and reunite once a week. I just ask that all of you who read this today would pray for the funding needed to continue the program at El Puente. Not for me, so that I will have a job opportunity—but for the people whose lives are day-by-day being improved and changed.

God Bless.

July 16th

One thin dime... Douglas found a dime on the beach today. We marveled at how it appeared to have shrunk substantially from what we remember. It was so thin, almost weightless. Each of us held the coin in our hand, tossing it, catching it, feeling it between our fingers. It felt ridiculously small.

The coins here are *heavy*. A gold-hued 500-colon coin is larger in diameter than a silver dollar and at least twice as thick. It's hard to carry more than a few in your pocket without looking somewhat weighed-down. We started throwing all the change in denominations of under 100 colones—the equivalent of about a quarter—into a Tupperware dish on the counter. I counted up about $8 worth yesterday and we estimate it weighs close to ten pounds.

The glow from within...I find solace in the red cut-glass hurricane lamp. It was given to me by a friend—un amante—last Christmas and unbelievably, made it all the way here with only a small chunk out of the base where it is not visible. I light a scented candle every night and watch the flickering flame against the fringes of darkness. It's therapeutic in a way; maybe because it is something familiar from my old life, maybe because of the memories it holds. As I write tonight, the lamp burns alongside me, calming my soul and igniting the spirit from within.

Chapter 19.
Off to School

July 18th

School daze... We had always wondered why the grade school changes its schedule so often. The concept of having half the kids attend mornings and the other half attend afternoons seemed to make sense—twice as many children can be taught that way. But why does this schedule alternate every other week? We're told it's because it allows for the children to 'sleep in' on the weeks they attend in the afternoons. When a teacher doesn't show up for class, the kids turn around and go home. No substitutes, no alternate plan. Just go home. Kind of like a snow day.

So half the kids attend mornings, and half attend afternoons. If your teacher isn't there, you get a day off. Ok, then why does the school schedule sometimes change mid-week, seemingly at the whim of the Director?

I went into Puerto Viejo to register my two children for school. As I had suspected, nobody really cared that they don't speak Spanish, or that we are most obviously not residents of this country. We walked right into the Director's office with no wait, and the only item he asked for was a copy of their last report cards to prove their grade levels.

We then met with the teachers to request a list of school supplies. A discussion ensued amongst them with regard to my two children. Their grade levels would dictate that one will attend mornings and the other, afternoons. This poses a problem for me due to the pressing need to find some kind of interim work.

In addition to wanting my children to attend on the same schedule, I also wanted them on a *specific* schedule—so they can attend with Alejandro and the gang. *No problema!* The teachers decided that tomorrow all the kids who were on a morning schedule today—Monday—would switch to afternoons for the remainder of the week. The afternoon kids would be switched to mornings. *We pretty much upset the entire schedule of an entire school and the decision was made without even consulting the Director.* ·

I am told that the United States currently has a literacy rate of 83%. Costa Rica's literacy rate is 93%. Maybe there is something to this.

School supplies... The list we were given at the school included many of the basics we luckily already had in stock—pens, pencils, colored pencils, and a pencil sharpener. The missing items included a few notebooks, two textbooks each, and the navy and white uniforms.

Thank goodness for Nanci. Lunch out and some gas money can in no way even begin to repay her for all the help she's given me—and today she outdid even herself. First, there was the trip into Puerto to introduce me to the Director, to help facilitate the conversation between the teachers and myself, and to use her somewhat stronger personality to push the issue of the same school schedule for the children.

The next stop was BriBri, where we were hoping to find everything we needed on the school supply list. Think again... We spent at least 45 minutes to an hour in the store where Nanci had successfully outfitted *each of the twenty-six BriBri children* she's helped to enroll in school. But with my little Americanos, the process took somewhat longer.

There's a distinct difference between the excitement of a child who's never been to school, who's never purchased school supplies, or had a decent pair of shoes—and the disdain of two children who in no way, shape or form, wished to go to public school, who have had their choice of every imaginable folder and notebook design at the local Wal-Mart, and who have never worn a pair of clunky 'sturdy' shoes.

In the end, the shoes were what took the longest. Each child tried on at least five or six pair—several times. We're talking basic black shoes. I believe the brand name on Douglas's was something akin to men's work boots in the U.S. They finally settled on a pair, although neither was completely satisfied with the purchase. In the same store, we found the white button-up uniform shirts and ended up buying them both a size larger than they normally wear—trying to err on the safe side. Then two pair of thick navy blue socks, the only kind in stock. No pants, no skirts, no books...

So we went on to Limon. The plan had been to take the public bus, but in the end, Nanci drove us by car. She showed us where the libreria was located, and we realized we've passed it many times before, on our way to the park. Luck was not with us though, as the libreria only had one of the four required schoolbooks in stock. We were advised a new shipment would arrive on Saturday.

After trying three or four clothing stores, and asking everyone we met on the street where we could buy school uniforms, we managed to find the pants and skirts. Douglas ended up with a size too large and the store ended up with an additional purchase of a belt that had to be cut down to fit him. Alex walked out with a smile—two pleated navy blue skirts in hand.

The afternoon wound down with lunch at Caribe Pizza and a stop at the pet store that landed us a beta, a home for the beta, and a small terrarium. Oh, and a stop at the appliance store, where we found a toaster oven for 13,000 colones. Trying to reheat pizza in a frying pan was just getting old...

We picked up Alejandro and his family half way home and gave them a lift to the edge of the Rainforest—as far as the car would go. We had picked up Daniel and his elderly mother earlier in the day on the way out of BriBri and carried them to Hone Creek. That's the way things are done around here—if you see somebody you know, you stop. *Sometimes right in the middle of the road.* Not to worry, everyone just goes around you.

Nanci stopped the car on the way to Limon to watch some howler monkeys carrying on in the treetops above us. One large black monkey had a tiny baby clinging to it's back, but try as we might, none of us could taunt them to howl. We were a sight—my kids hanging out the windows, car doors wide open. As expected, the buses went around us, the trucks went around us, and the cars went around us...*lucky for us.*

July 19th

The first school day...Wrought with apprehension, both on the kid's part and my own. The feeling was glum as we started out toward the pulperia in the sprinkling rain. We were waiting for Alejandro, et al, and soon spotted them peering through the hazy windows of Nanci's passing car. She fit us all in—two adults and six kids. Me, with my hip up on the handle of the door, Alejandro sitting on the gearshift, and Douglas on my lap in the front seat.

The arrival at the school was somewhat daunting. Nanci dropped us at the curb, leaving me entirely on my own this time. The report cards were taken in to the Director as requested, and I managed to bluff my way through the conversation. I then made a feeble attempt to explain Douglas's peanut allergy to his unsmiling bilingual teacher and was finally satisfied as she shoved the package of Benedryl and the Epipen into her desk.

Douglas had not quite settled down from his unpleasant 'episode' prior to leaving home this morning, and had the mannerism of a bull ready to lock horns with the first unlucky one to make eye contact. In contrast, Alex was fully composed, smiling sweetly, and loving how she looked in the new pleated skirt. She willingly posed for photos with Maria and Carmelita.

Alex and Maria at the Escuela Publica

With the unexpected ride into town, we had arrived nearly an hour early. Morning classes were still in session, so we sat down on a concrete wall and watched—and waited. My first observation was that this was very unlike any school I'd ever seen. There was one long building with four classrooms in a row. All open air—only bars and space on either side. There were no doors hanging in the classroom doorways. A lunchroom held four picnic tables and the tempting smell of fried chicken wafted through. A heavy-set Caribbean woman who appeared to be the cook peered through an open window.

Chaos. The utter chaos was what struck me first. Boys around the age of ten were hitting, punching, and chasing each other all around with a stick and an umbrella. Oddly enough, it seemed par for the course, as they all appeared to be grinning from ear to ear. The little girls were walking around much in the way little girls do, chattering, whispering, casting shy glances our way. Back in Florida, every student was required to walk in a quiet and orderly fashion along a blue line painted on the sidewalk. Here, nobody was on the blue line. *In fact, there was no blue line...*

There is only one photocopier in town, so I was directed to take the children's original report cards to ATEC, the utility company, to have the copies made. One of the children's teachers requested that I purchase a legal size red folder at ATEC and bring it back to her by the afternoon, laminated and with a clip to hold the child's records.

The lady at ATEC was none too friendly and directed me with a backward flip of her hand to the shelf near a darkened corner of the room. It turned out to be lined with miscellaneous office supplies. She refused, however, to laminate the folder even as I insisted the teacher at the Escuela Publica had informed me that every other parent's folder had been laminated there. No, it's much too big for the machine—but you can purchase a sheet of plastic and do it yourself. So tomorrow I will return to the school with the lopsided copies in the red folder with plastic taped to the outside.

Douglas showed up at the Internet Café at 3:45 pm, five minutes before school was supposed to have let out. When asked how he found me there, he informed me that *he just took a wild guess* at where I would be. In the meantime, Alex was left standing at the school entrance all by herself.

This evening was the first time the kids didn't actually have to be chased into the shower. They were eager to shed the heavy shoes and uniforms and spent the rest of the evening running around the house in underpants. Uniforms were washed and hung, and we sat down and discussed their day. What did they learn?

I was very surprised to find that my children had learned many things their first day in this Spanish-speaking school. Alex's teacher had asked each child in the classroom to say something to her in English, phrases taken from their weekly English lesson. She found the situation to be similar to one she had encountered before when she attended school in Florida with Spanish-speaking children who had just entered the country. Except this time she was on the other end of the spectrum. She came home with a beautiful picture of a frog that she had copied off the board and colored. And a story to go with it—also copied off the board. Although she didn't have a clue what it said.

Douglas's lessons were a bit more basic. He learned that 'callate' means 'shut up' and 'silencio' means silence. And if someone persistently hits you and you break down and hit him back, he will eventually stop. He also learned that 'Mi nombre es' means 'My name is...' and that you must write inside the lines, and write EXACTLY the same size as the teacher wants, or your work will be considered no good for that day, and discarded into the trash receptacle.

I learned that life goes on. That the perception of this horribly traumatic experience turned out to be just that—a perception. Granted, the school days here are going to be different. Recess is held twice a day, rather than once a week. Kids are kids and the school curriculum is not geared toward passing a standardized test. The main subjects taught are Spanish, English and Math. A little Social Studies and Science for the older children.

Last week, Alejandro and Maria came home with a worksheet all about stop lights and how they work and how the traffic flows, or should flow. Why was this concept being taught to second graders who don't yet drive and will probably never drive? *So that they can learn to cross the street safely.* No matter that this town has never had a stop light and probably never will.

July 20th

In my day, we used to walk to school, five miles, uphill, in the snow…The familiar old adage many of our parents used to tell us now rings true. I actually walk three kilometers under the pounding sun, with choking dust, or in the pouring rain, four times a day—to take the kids to and from school. Usually carrying both their backpacks in addition to my own bag. And three water bottles. Next week they are going to start walking on their own.

Today it was a deluge. I managed to avoid the rain for the most part as I arrived home after dropping the children off for class, but by the time school let out, it was pouring. With umbrella and the kid's rain ponchos in hand, I made the trek toward town. No dust today, only great big mud puddles that splatter everywhere when a car goes by. Despite the umbrella, I was soaked by the time I arrived. Although it seemed unfathomable, the wind appeared to be picking up some of the ocean water and spraying it all the way up onto the highway. I wished I'd had the foresight to wear my slicker as well.

Alejandro and his siblings didn't seem to be ready to leave school, or perhaps they were hoping Nanci would come for them as she often does when it rains. I was sure they were correct, so we set out on our own for the house. A little boy named Jordan seemed to be keeping time with us as we left the school grounds, so I let him in under my umbrella. It turns out he lives at Playa Negra as well, only a few hundred meters shy of our house. He was happy to keep dry and I think we made a new amigo.

Alex is sure her teacher told her there is no school now until next Tuesday. At least that was what she understood of the message that was translated. So tomorrow only Douglas will go to school, and Alex will accompany me to the Stevens to help cut vegetables. The boy who kept punching Douglas yesterday was moved across the room and things seem to have settled down on that front. Douglas pointed the boy out to me this morning and I gave him a very stern, knowing look. It's unlikely my child will be bothered again for a while—at least not by the same boy.

Alex brought home three notebook pages today, copied from the board, very little of which we were able to translate—at least in a way that made sense. She said it was a song—the class had sung it. It looks to be a sad, tragic story about how the seasons come and go. Two hours later, and we're still working on making sense of the words.

The trauma of the day was when Alex learned that each day next week she will be required to read a story out of her Spanish book—during class—and then write a report on it—in Spanish. I tried to explain to her again the reasons for her school attendance, none of which have anything remotely to do with academic excellence. She's still worried about how she will accomplish this task. We've decided our goal for the next five days will be to work on the alphabet and correct pronunciation so that Alex will be able to read the story aloud if she is called on, even if she has no clue what she is reading. *Poco a poco...*

Chapter 20.
Reflections

Oh so Blue... We named the beta Azul and he's still floating around in the little purple tank with the little purple rocks—belly down, which is a good sign. He survived an hour or more walking around Limon as we shopped on Monday, another forty-five minutes in the car, a fifteen minute stop as we picked up Alejandro's family, and then the walk from the car to the house. Pretty sturdy little fellow. He is mostly blue with a tail that fades to red—much like Flounder from our past life. But they do change colors you know. Flounder did—several times.

Cesspool anyone? I overheard a conversation this morning as I sat in a trendy little local café, specializing in 'special' brownies and health food. The young couple that owns the place has a three-month old baby, who happens to have come down with a fever. The discussion was regarding the sanitary conditions in town, or lack thereof, and several friends of theirs who have recently taken ill.

I must admit that Puerto Viejo is not the cleanest place I've ever lived, but it does have a certain character. One learns to avoid the mesh garbage holding areas anywhere from Saturday until Tuesday garbage pickup—or Wednesday, whenever the garbage truck gets around to coming through. And the children have learned to stop catching guppies in what they first thought was a little river running from nearby homes onto the beach—until our new friend from New York commented on the brownish film floating on top of the water. We started to notice a lot of little runoffs like this, right in the middle of town, and have since gathered that Puerto has not yet gotten the hang of sanitary sewage disposal. No treatment facilities here. Just a puddle in the back yard.

July 21st

School news...Alex is off school now for three days, reasons unknown. Douglas rode his bike the three kilometers into town this morning by himself. We checked on him later to be sure he actually *went to school,* and there he was on the playground, standing underneath some sort of fruit tree with the rest of the class. Several boys were throwing rocks at the tree, apparently in an attempt to bring down whatever was growing on it. Must have been snack time.

Jungle Lodge here we come...whether we like it or not. We were informed by Colocha today that the agreement she had made with us at the beginning of our rental contract is no longer valid. Mauricio's family members have been staying in the vacant house that used to belong to his mother and they've decided to stay through the month of August. This was the house we were supposed to have been moved into.

Colocha seemed willing to try to find a solution to the dilemma and suggested we might like to spend thirteen days on a 'vacation' of sorts at the Jungle Nature Lodge, which is owned by her daughter. I voiced my only concern, that being to drag everything we own in the world halfway across town will be nearly impossible on foot. We were relieved when an offer was extended that would allow us to store the majority of our belongings here in a locked room of the family's house.

My thoughts on the matter are mixed. In a perfect world, we would not end up having to move. Some twist of fate will have changed the plans of the people who will be intruding upon our lives to stay in this rental home for part of the month of August. This is, unfortunately, not a perfect world, so I must concede and choose to learn from the experience. A free stay at the Nature Lodge in the rainforest really is quite an opportunity. Of course, Colocha touted all of the advantages of such a stay, and did not once mention boa constrictors, vipers or scorpions. She did say we would have the run of the lodge facility itself, which is normally rented out to large groups, rather than putting us up in one of the small cabinas. I did the only thing I could, and agreed to go along with the plan. More to come...

Reflections...A full moon has been rising slowly and now sits staring squarely at the house. The stars are quite visible tonight with not a cloud in sight. Although it was a very hot day—as compared to yesterday's rainy respite from the sun—the air is now cool. Cooler than expected, and very, very still. A dog barks off in the distance and the waves crash rhythmically onto the beach.

My own children are fast asleep in their beds, exhausted from the day's activities. I realized today that the structure to be found in public school is a good thing. Spending the day with Alex, who was suddenly jolted out of her new routine, and Douglas, whose week has remained constant, has cemented the belief that children need and thrive on structure.

Mauricio was having a conversation with Douglas when we finally caught up with him near the house on the return trip from school today. He was explaining to him how it is best to just sit back in school, relax, listen to what is being said, and not worry, not fret about what he doesn't understand.

All babies speak the same language when they are born but each child then goes on to learn the language spoken most often around them. Alejandro has been in school now for one full school year. He was nine when he started school and when he moved here from Talamanca, he spoke only the indigenous language of BriBri. Now, only a year later, he is able to communicate entirely in Spanish.

It will all come, in time.

July 22nd

Paquitas...I was looking for spaghetti sauce the other day and finally asked the clerk for some assistance. She pointed to the top shelf to a box of packets about the length and width of an individual Tang, but slightly fatter. They even sat lined up in a sideways cardboard carton, much like Tang. So I grabbed a handful—con hongos—with mushrooms. It took six full packets to cover the meatballs I had made in our smallest saucepan, scarcely equaling a small jar of Prego.

Milk and OJ come standard in one-liter shelf cartons. I'm not exactly sure of the conversion, but I am sure at least four or five liters would fit into a U.S. gallon. Aspirin is sold over the counter at Jeffrey's—by the pill. Soap is always sold in individual bars, and butter is *sold by the stick*.

Why the small paquitas? Could have something to do with the way everyone shops here—pretty much daily. I haven't completely figured out the reason for the daily shopping routine. All I know is that the majority of people can be seen walking to the store in the morning for milk and eggs, and back in the afternoon for staples to prepare the evening meal. You buy what you need for the day and no more.

One theory for this phenomenon is perhaps simply force of habit. I recall many years ago visiting a friend in Limon who didn't have a refrigerator. Even today, none of the indigenous people have electricity, let alone appliances. So daily shopping has for many always been a thing of necessity. The people who are fortunate enough to have a refrigerator usually get by with an apartment-size model that must be defrosted every other day—the only type available for purchase here.

I suspect that a visit to Wal-Mart will probably bring with it a bit of culture shock after living in mini-everything world.

July 23rd

Libros? Not here...Where oh where will we find the schoolbooks for class? We've been all around Puerto, we've been to BriBri, and we've been to Limon—twice. Scouting around Puerto for the books was not a big deal. And Alex and I made an afternoon of a bus trip into BriBri while Douglas was in school Friday.

The trips to Limon are a little more complicated. We took the first with Nanci on Monday, and the other this afternoon—just after Soup Kitchen—by bus. The libreria that had promised us a shipment of books today said they don't have the books we need in stock and won't be getting them in. Try another libreria across town...

We struck up a conversation with some young men peddling ink pens of all things and they actually took the time to walk us a few blocks over to the other book store. Unfortunately, the metal sheets had been pulled down over the windows and padlocked, a sure sign the place was closed.

We had gone through a lot to get to Limon this afternoon. The soup kitchen, although a labor of love, is admittedly tiring—and very hot. Sue has left for Mexico, and Alejandro Grande did not show, so we were left a few hands short. A bus trip to Limon when one has not just awoken completely refreshed is not a pleasant experience. It was 1:30 pm when the bus came by, perfect timing as far as the bus schedule goes, but not perfect timing for overtired children.

I won't explain in any kind of detail what happened the next five kilometers. Only that out of respect for the other passengers, I was forced to pull the cord at Hone Creek, only a few miles down the road, and quickly disembark with my arms wrapped around an unruly boy. We started walking back toward Puerto in the baking sun—no shade at 1:40 pm—then a sudden change in attitude prompted me to give it one more try. We turned around and sat down at the Hone Creek bus shelter and waited. Another bus to Limon passed by within minutes, and luck was with us as we caught a ride on it.

Tomorrow will be my third trip to Limon in a week. Barry and Nanci have invited me to take their ritual Sunday drive with them, and I enjoy spending time with other adults on Sundays while my children spend time with their dad.

Barry has promised to show me a store that I simply must become familiar with—something about computer supplies, ribbons—important stuff. I'm looking forward to my day off.

Chapter 21.
Life is Good

Flashlight bugs…We used to chase fireflies as kids. One of my greatest memories of childhood is of running around the yard barefoot in the dark with thick green grass underneath our feet, chasing the fireflies with an open mayonnaise jar in hand. In rural Pennsylvania, these insects were plentiful in the summer months, particularly around the 4th of July.

I woke up the other night to find a light making it's way up one side of my mosquito net and down the other. Flashing every so often. Only rather than a tiny little flash of white light, the light from this guy more resembled a car with one neon green headlight. The beam emanating from what we lovingly refer to as 'flashlight bugs' created a hazy half circle around the insect itself, much brighter than any I'd ever seen before.

In my half-asleep state, it hadn't occurred to me to turn on the light and inspect the bug itself. Just a firefly…I found out quite by accident, many days later, that the big brown two-inch beetles that we had considered a nuisance and swatted off the beds covers are really our nightlight buddies. Try fitting more than one of them in a mayonnaise jar!

July 25th

Could it be??? Maxi Bodega—The store was a Sam's Club copycat right down to the electronics lining the shelves just inside the door, up until the final stop at the cash register where I was asked if I had a membership card. Ok, maybe Sam's Club is a little stretch of the imagination. Perhaps Big Lots would be a more appropriate tienda in comparison. In any event, I left the store 50,000 colones poorer and with eight bolsas in hand.

Autonomy... The kids have begun to gain a bit of independence, riding their bicycles to Jeffrey's for bread and milk, and to the motel where their dad lives to visit. Tomorrow, they will bike it into school at 6:30 am and I'll trust them to actually get there. Douglas made the trip himself last week and we were pleased to see him sitting in class as we passed by later in the afternoon. A brief premonition of him sitting on the old barge at the edge of town with fishing pole in hand had passed through my mind momentarily as he rode out of the driveway that morning.

Bastante? In the diccionario, the word bastante refers to 'enough' as in—I've had enough. Apparently, as many words in the Spanish language, it also has a dual meaning. A friend recently told me a story about an experience he had in a local restaurant. He had held up his hand and said 'bastante' and each time he did so, the waitress, rather than ceasing to bring food, kept bringing more...and more...The looser interpretation of 'bastante'—at least while seated in a restaurant—is "No, I haven't had enough yet..."

Joyce the Juice Queen—also a talented artist... Joyce is the retired lady who lives a few meters down the road toward town. Sick of the hurricanes, she picked up and moved here a year or so ago from Sarasota, Florida. On Saturdays, Joyce is the 'Juice Queen' at El Puente. She stands by the massive metal pot that takes up most of the dining room table, pouring and mixing enough hand-squeezed juice for nearly 100 people.

During the week, Joyce is a budding artist. Her craft is ceramic jewelry, in the most brilliant colors and designs, and she can often be spotted sitting along the roadside near Hot Rocks Café peddling her wares—at least when La Policia aren't policing the area. She was shut down unexpectedly the other afternoon at the whim of the unpredictable police force for lack of the necessary permit. Luckily, a local restaurant owner took a liking to Joyce's jewelry and has promised to put up a glass display in his place where she will be able to sell her treasures at four or five times what she can get on the street. Needless to say, Christmas presents sent back home this year will most likely be a-la-Joyce.

July 25th Second Entry

We got the beat...The music is always there, subtly pushing through ones consciousness. It has a certain rhythm, sometimes even the same refrain repeated over and over again—but it's never really *intolerable*. The notes float around in the air, mixing and becoming a part of the breeze. They hold a gentle swaying rhythm, soothing, blending well with the ocean sounds.

Sitting in the house, it is always heard as a distant chant, barely distinguishable. Even without a calendar, it's easy to know when the weekend has rolled around as every radio is turned up a notch and dozens of voices can be heard from every direction.

As one approaches the intersection near Jeffrey's, the music becomes louder, blaring from gigantic speakers at the corner bar. The music emanating from the many restaurants and bars downtown becomes a gigantic glob of sound from Friday night to Sunday, when tourists and Ticos from all over frequent our usually quiet town.

Puerto is a party spot, for sure. There has been many a time when the car or bus we were riding in got stuck on the main street, wedged in between the other vehicles. It's impossible to skirt the main drag, as it's the only road into and out of town. Another reason I've been putting off purchasing a car of our very own.

Bye, Bye Bus Stop... Sunday morning as we made our usual trip into town, we found the bus shelter near Jeffrey's laying in a crumpled heap on the ground. Telltale skid marks and signs of red paint are the only clues to this pressing mystery.

Nobody knows if and when the shelter will be reconstructed. I'm told every bus shelter in the country is the product of either a concerted effort on the part of the community or a gratuitous act of a local business owner. This particular shelter had been put up by Jeffrey—or at least paid for by Jeffrey—and not only served as a place to wait for the bus, but as an all-around gathering place, a resting place, and a place to just hang out when one felt like it. *I noticed the front stoop of Jeffrey's corner store was uncharacteristically crowded this morning.*

July 27th

Books at last! I sent notes in with the kids this morning explaining to each of their teachers why they still don't have the required books. Every bookstore we've been to has been out of the books and won't order any more until the next school year begins—in February. Of course, that rule can be bent, but only if we wish to purchase ten copies of each title.

So Douglas came home with his teacher's book today and we took it to ATEC, the local utility company, to have a copy made. Our order was completed just before closing time. However, since it was copied single-sided and on thicker paper, he now has a 'book' about three times as thick as the original, and unbound. Lucky for us, there is a store vaguely described to be located 'somewhere in BriBri' that can punch holes and put in a spiral binding.

More on books...I happened to mention to Mauricio the trouble we've been having obtaining books for the children. No problema! His sister is a teacher and thinks she may be able to find the books we need in San Jose this weekend.

July 28th

Ka-Boom! Last night we had a storm. Thunder, lightning, the whole bit. I think the teachers must have been watching the weather channel, because the kids were told not to come to class today. A thunderstorm in our new home is *a little bit different* from the storms we usually slept through when we lived in Florida. The rain pounds the tin roof, the heavy upstairs shutters must be closed against the force of the wind, and then there is 'the drip' to contend with. For some reason, I awaken when the rain begins and don't fall back asleep until exhaustion overcomes me, usually close to dawn. Another theory is that I've been hitting the Vanilla Nuez café a little too heavily lately...

Mauricio came over a few days ago with a large roll of silver tape in hand and said he was here to fix the roof. He climbed the two stories on the tallest ladder I've ever seen—made of sturdy bamboo poles lashed together with rope. Amazingly, the tape held fast during the night and we no longer have a puddle in the middle of the bedroom the morning after a rain.

This morning we awakened to face a familiar dilemma. All of the laundry lining the clothesline and the side railings of the house has been wet for three days and of course, is even wetter still with the additional rainfall. There is not much of a chance it will dry out any time soon. I'm told during the rainy season nothing ever dries and that's easy to believe. The plan is to take all the towels and sheets in to the Laundromat today and then start taking the rest in shifts throughout the week. Maybe by the weekend we can restart the cycle again and get back into the 'regular' laundry routine, which involves hand washing at least twice a day and hanging during the hottest hours so everything dries by nightfall.

As I lay awake during the night listening to the sheets of rain pummeling the house, I could not help but think of Alejandro and his siblings, huddled together on a blanket in the corner of their wooden platform. Surely, they must be soaking wet, as rain was blowing into our own living room, turning the wooden furniture and floors a dark chocolate brown. It's no wonder little Alejandro suffers from chronic pulmonary problems. I now understand a little better the close-knit group these children have formed, as their lifestyle demands that they depend one upon the other.

The missing tooth... Douglas woke up the other morning with a loose bottom tooth. He tried to no avail to pull it using a piece of string. The lack of doorknobs in the house was unfortunately, somewhat of a deterrent to the age-old trick. He finally worked the tooth out on the way to the bus stop and carried it in his pocket to Limon.

The owner of Caribe Pizza was the first to be treated to a peek at the bloody tooth. Luckily, he had not actually sat down to join us for lunch. 'Buena suerte!' he told Douglas. Great luck!

The entire day, the children pondered the validity of the Tooth Fairy and finally decided that if she puts American money under Douglas's pillow tonight, this is surely a sign that she is indeed Real. Since they were under the impression I have only colones left in my possession, this would be the ultimate test to determine whether Mom and the Tooth Fairy are one and the same.

The next morning was joyous as Douglas found two shiny quarters lying underneath his pillow. I'm just not ready yet to give up the mysticism that goes hand-in-hand with early childhood.

July 29th

A Case of Mistaken Identity... The fuzzy little creature crawled across the kitchen floor with a sense of purpose. He moved slowly, just enough to irritate me as I was preparing the kids to leave for school by 6:30 am With broom raised, I aimed to squash the little nuisance. But Alex yelled at the last minute "No, Mommy, it's a baby crab!!!" Thus saving his life. Well, at that time of the morning, he *looked* like a tarantula, the only creature I can bring myself to terminate with no reserve. So baby crabby lives, scurrying back and forth across the living room floor where the kids left him. He'll be my companion for a while this morning, until the kids return from school.

They've returned...7:12 am The morning was short-lived. As happens quite often, Douglas found out when he got to school there will be no class again today. Barry is working on a system to resolve this nagging issue. Perhaps the school's director can post a notice on the Internet so Barry in turn can tack a note up at Jeffrey's corner store and on the side of their house where the indigenous children make their first stop on the way into town. For now, there is no other choice but to live with the unpredictable school schedule.

Hot, Hot, Hot... Looking on the bright side—the laundry IS drying. And the kids stopped at their dad's and decided to stay on for a bit...probably for the best, considering my present temperament. The thermometer says 78 F but it must be lying. In the direct sunlight of the living room, it feels more like 98 F. Fluffy white clouds are sporadically drifting across the path of its heated rays, causing a fluctuation in temperature every so often, but not enough to really make a difference. The horses clomping down the path behind the house are neighing loudly, possibly bothered by the flies, or the heat, or both. I'm watching the chapear, and wondering how he can stand the heat, decked out in a heavy vinyl body suit and head covering. He kind of resembles a firefighter in full gear and I imagine he feels like one too.

July 30th

Buzzzzzz...I awoke to find a gigantic bumblebee buzzing loudly inside my mosquito net. And three blobs of orange sticky something on my sheet and left arm. The substance was akin to pine sap and won't come off no matter how hard I scrub. Our theory is that that bee left this gift for me; some sort of nectar brought in from a nearby flower.

Butterfly migration? Yesterday during dinner, we suddenly noticed flocks—or is it swarms?—of butterflies, flying over the house. All moving in the same direction, roughly South. Such a phenomenon this was, that we got up from the dinner table and hung over the side of the living room wall to watch. At first, these dark spots high up in the sky appeared to be tiny birds, all hatched at once. Then the fluttering of their wings looked to us more like fruit bats. Finally, one of the wayward creatures fluttered in the wrong direction, toward the roof of the house, and we realized they were indeed giant black and green butterflies.

The Future is Ours...I can still see the vision of The Bridge, as it will be someday. The new buildings. The office where my desk will sit. The children's craft and play area. Shower facilities. The new, larger kitchen where several hands will work together to prepare for the weekly soup kitchen. I haven't given up hope of God's plan for me here and still believe it is somehow connected to the Stevens and El Puente. Some evenings, I reread the dozens of entries I made in the Journal, all the way from the beginning of this adventure, when it was just a seed in my mind. And I'm reminded that surely this was meant to be.

Alex has stopped talking about wanting to go back to Florida. Now she talks about 'when we get into a more permanent house', or she conjures up elaborate plans in her mind of crafts we could make (like Joyce) to sell at the market or on the roadside in case the job doesn't materialize soon enough—"So that we can stay here, mommy..."

Douglas does the same things he did in Florida—chases lizards, plays outdoors, and rides his bicycle. Life is not much different for him here, there is just more of it. Sometimes he gets overdone, overtired. The long bike rides into Puerto, the afternoons at the Bridge, it's a lot for a seven-year old. He's learning to adapt. Slowly learning what is acceptable and what will no longer be tolerated. In some ways, school actually seems to be more difficult for him than for Alex, although she was the one who fought it the most in the beginning.

We're learning the academic side of school here is less complex. The teacher walks out of the room several times a day, and when the kids get too bored, they begin to chant, "Teacher, teacher..." They cheer when she announces a day off from school, probably more because these announcements are unexpected, rather than infrequent. It's a different environment that simply can't be compared to the old way. School days are four hours long on a good day, as compared to ten hours, including aftercare, to which the children had been accustomed.

Some things we don't understand and probably never will. We just accept them and many times realize later that they really do make sense. Much more common sense is used here, such as telling the kids no school tomorrow when it looks like a heavy rain.

Just last week Alex said to me, "I'm never going to learn anything at school mommy, because I don't want to learn, and with that attitude—I won't..." She's a smart little girl. But that statement was somehow a turning point in her relationship with herself and her decision to adapt to this new environment. Now, both kids practice saying the vowels in Spanish—*ah, eh, ih, oh, oooh.* And they mix many phrases into their everyday play without even thinking about it. We all do. I suppose this is a part of the process. Helping them with their homework is reinforcing the basics of Spanish grammar for me, as well, and I'm picking up things here and there that weren't taught in the textbooks or phrases that were never mentioned on the learning cassettes. I find myself more and more joining in the conversations on Saturday afternoons with Daniel and Maria and feel as if I'm beginning to fit in as part of the Bridge 'group'.

Un desfile? Alex had a surprise Friday morning when the kids were pulled from school after breakfast to march in an impromptu parade down the main street in town. Apparently, every few months, a campaign is launched to spread 'Dengue Awareness' and its focus is mainly on the children. The parade was led by an ambulance with flashing lights, followed by the school children who responded with a loud "Dengue!" to whatever question was being asked them by the adult walking along side the group.

Pamphlets were passed out, describing how to prevent the spread of dengue, through eliminating standing water in old tires, overturned bricks, etc. The focus was on every person looking around their yard, and their own personal environment, in order to eliminate potential breeding grounds for mosquitoes. Not a bad idea.

Do we live on an anthill? We had another one of those 'unexpected' events this afternoon upon arriving home to find millones de 'ants' in the kitchen. As it turns out, the crazy ants—thank goodness it was the crazy ants and not the 'others', since this variety doesn't actually bite—the crazy ants feel it necessary after every long rain to pack up and carry their eggs to safety. So literally thousands, if not millions of them swarm into the nearest structure. Last time, it was our bathroom where we found the shower covered with a moving black blanket. This time, we were less fortunate, as it was our kitchen that was invaded.

We first noticed the ants moving on the canned and packaged food that sits on the only shelf in the kitchen. Then, the moving wall of ants extended behind the shelf, covering all the countertops and dishes. Closer inspection revealed the entire back wall of the house was covered with egg-carrying ants pouring through every crack and crevice. We quickly moved everything out of the way and went through another can of Raid, spraying first the inside, then the outside walls of the house. Alex noticed the ants crawling up the side of the house and wisely went to check their bedroom where the infestation continued on the wall behind Douglas's bed.

In the end, we swept out quite a mound of dead ants once the Raid fog settled. We're all a little lightheaded this evening from the unexpected fumigation. But I think the job is done. The kitchen is much cleaner, much more organized, and we got a feel for what it will be like repacking the house for the move next week…

August 1st

School blues…The days seem to get longer and longer. This morning, Alex awoke with a headache and a sore throat, and Douglas suddenly developed the same symptoms when he found out his sister wouldn't be going to school. By 9 am everyone was fine so we took a ride into town to print out the prized sloth picture—the one taken the very day after we arrived. ATEC laminated it for a few hundred colones and we now have a new addition to the children's bedroom wall.

We found out later in the day that the Segundo—second grade—actually had afternoon class today, beginning at 11:30 am and ending around 3:45 pm. However, Alex brought home a note from her teacher last Thursday, stating her class—Cuarto—was to resume on Monday at 7 am. The plan before they had been proclaimed ill this morning had been for them to go in for morning session.

Tomorrow is a national holiday, so of course, there will be no school. Wednesday is a mystery and I'm debating whether it would be prudent for me to just walk both children in at 7 am and then walk *whoever doesn't have school* back home again...The pressing question, though, is how I will deal with this mixed-up school schedule once I begin working.

August 1st Second Entry

There seem to be two types of sunset pictures—color and black and white. Tonight, the photos are in color. Brilliant hues of fiery red pulled up and out through the top of the clouds create a watercolor portrait spread against the backdrop of the sea. The pictures never do the sunset justice, but serve as a simple reminder to trigger the true glory deep within the mind's eye.

August 2nd

Three bottles of glitter glue...money well spent. I've said it a million times, and I'll say it again. Give a kid a bottle of glue, a couple crayons and a sheet of paper—and in this case, a cup full of seashells—and watch a masterpiece unfold.

Organization does wonders for creativity. Now that all of the craft materials sit together in one cardboard box—thanks to the package from my parents last month—the kids spend way more time doing 'projects' and that means less time fighting...thank goodness for glitter glue!

Hace fresco esta mañana—only 74 F and it's already 9:00 am. We've learned to revel in small miracles and this definitely qualifies. The cleaning lady is making her rounds and I'm getting ready to clear out and take the bus into BriBri. With the holiday today, I'm not really sure the bus is actually running, but that will be another one of those learning experiences. In any case, I'll sit at what's left of the bus stop and wait.

Mountain air... As I sat waiting for the return bus this afternoon, I pondered the differences between Playa Negra and BriBri. The latter is completely surrounded by the Talamanca mountain range, and this day, as is typical, steamy clouds hung just above the thick vegetation. Today, for the first time, I was treated to the sounds of the infamous howler monkeys. They seemed to be out in great numbers as the entire hillside echoed with their cries. While I stood waiting for the photocopy of Douglas's schoolbook to be spiral bound, I spied a bright green iguana and a poison whiptail—two additional species I'd thus far seen only in books. Most stores here are set up as storefronts, where one walks up and stands at an open window while the work, such as photocopying, is completed.

BriBri has nothing of the feel of the Caribbean coastal town of Puerto Viejo. In a tropical kind of way, it resembles the small town in North Carolina where my parents will soon retire. The tranquility of the surrounding mountain range and the unmistakably different sounds of nature is calming and adds somewhat to its charm.

August 3rd

Gray Skies... It seems the lingering rains sometimes bring with them a deflated feeling that can be transmitted even as one passes another on a bicycle. Someone once said the sun has a lot to do with moods and I tend to agree. Even in paradise, the gray skies and constant drip, drip occasionally dulls the spirit. Knowing the alternative is the heat of mid-day, we should be grateful for the fresh clean air that blows in with the storm. But, somehow the mente is set up to read different signals. It stubbornly refuses to revel in the coolness—instead remaining steadfast in the darkness clinging to the day.

August 5th

Aire fresco...I try to imagine myself back in the U.S. during a rainstorm, versus sitting here in the open house. With the exception of the hurricane season, when we sat for three days in darkness with the windows open and the winds whipping through, I don't think I can recall any other time we *really listened* to a storm. The closest I came to nature were the camping trips with my oldest son, Jonathan, during his early childhood years, but nothing much in the past decade. We'd become stagnant, impervious to the wonders of nature and the tactile sensations of a good rain. Perhaps one of the many lessons I will take with me from this experience is the ability to more thoroughly enjoy what God has created.

On the flip side, I worry in the back of my mind about the small child who will soon be making his way home along the beach road in the downpour. His afternoon class started at 10:00 am today, rather than 11:00, and one never knows whether that will mean dismissal an hour earlier. If so, he will be coming down the path at any moment, on the rickety bicycle that can be heard from a quarter mile away. And inevitably, looking like a drown rat in need of a hot shower and a cup of cocoa.

10 minutes later... Our speculations on the arrival of Douglas from school were correct. He resembled a slippery, wet mongoose as he stepped out of waterlogged shoes. He stated that there were lots of 'drips' in the classroom today. The children, in fact, had to rearrange their desks—several times—in an effort to keep dry; and Douglas found it amusing that the largest drip was directly over the teacher's head.

We Miss Blockbuster! I learned today another lesson on rules and regulations and how certain things are viewed, depending upon which neck of the woods you live in. Take copyright laws for example, and the penalties thereof. I thought it odd the other day that the local utility office had no problem whatsoever when asked to photocopy an entire textbook. As long as we paid the 20 colones per page, copyright *no esta importante.*

We stopped in at the local video rental store today. The first thing we noticed was the wall behind the *caja,* full of what appeared to be original DVD's taped up in a haphazard display of sorts, each printed with a large three-digit number in black permanent marker.

The DVD's for rent were, of course, not the originals. We perused the photocopied DVD jackets and chose two children's movies. Then, the cashier went to a large black book of the rental copies and pulled the corresponding discs out, slapping them into a broken generic rental jacket. We paid the equivalent of $5 each for a *deposito,* and $2 for the rental itself. No membership card to show, just give your first name. The incentive to return the DVD's is, of course, tied to the hefty loss of the *deposito.*

Batty # 5... Another bat in the bedroom this evening. This one was larger than the average fruit bat and unusual in one way. Rather than flying in and out of the upstairs rooms, it flew in, and then landed. Closer inspection revealed the little mammal, with outstretched wings, resting comfortably on the far side of Alex's pink mosquito netting. *"Mommy, get that thing off my bed!"* my daughter demanded. I approached it with camera in hand, only to be hissed at as a vampire would hiss at its would-be prey. No more up-close and personal with these little guys, no matter how cute they might be.

August 6th

Bicicletas por Venta... Another bout with the bicycle woes and a decision was made. I had spied miniature versions of my sturdy beach cruiser the other day in BriBri; unfortunately, I had no way to transport them back to Puerto. After Douglas's most recent tantrum over a broken chain, I sent him packing—to see if his dad could borrow a truck to bring home some new bicycles. He had, in fact, in his fit of temper, already packed up and was dragging his suitcase down the stairs when I intercepted.

Later in the afternoon, I haggled with a salesman and managed to reduce the final price tag about 5,000 colones, equivalent to a ten-dollar break for the two. I'm hoping the new bicycles will reduce the stress level a little bit around here. The highlight of *my day* was when my daughter advised me I should teach daddy to say "I don't speak Spanish" in Spanish, because, as she explained, "He just sits there and stares when someone is talking to him, mommy." It's the little things...

We managed to find a hotel in town that actually has Jacuzzi bathtubs, so Alex will have her wish for a 'real' bath on her birthday. Then, the next morning, we'll set out for our new temporary home, 100 meters down the road past the Stevens, and, the part that wasn't originally mentioned—another 100 meters up the path into the Rainforest. I have a feeling this is where the real adventure begins.

August 7th

Downtown on a rainy day... The best part about shopping along the beachfront is the prices. Necklaces for $2 and $3, colorful hand-woven shoulder bags for a few dollars more, and your choice of restaurants where you can stop in for a 'casado'. Literally translated—a casado—is a married man. Otherwise known as a typical luncheon consisting of rice, beans, and your choice of fish, chicken, or beef. Topped off with a glass of fresh mango—mon-goh—juice, I've found this to be an exquisite way to sit out an afternoon shower.

The family who runs this particular Soda was hanging out underneath the tin roof—chattering, laughing. Several older women were in the kitchen, stirring with gigantic spoons. A couple of forty-something men could be seen helping out on the interior as well. Two of the children practiced saying the menu in English as a teenaged brother wrote it out in colorful chalk on the board near the entrance. Cheeken, feesh, esnapper...No—quita la 'e'. *Don't pronounce the 'e'.* Esnapper. Ok, she finally got it on about the fifth try, but put forth a very good effort I might say. No wonder most of the kids here are bilingual.

Riding a bicycle in the rain really isn't so bad. In fact, if you can get past the wet hair and learn how to blink both eyes at the same time to keep the droplets out, it's actually quite pleasurable. Someone told me the other day that the reason all the maids around here are so—I believe he used the word 'buff'—is the three-to-five-mile a day bicycle ride to and from work. I still don't think the women can compare to the strength of a Chapear, though, with their rippling abs and bulging biceps. And there's just something about a man with a machete…

Esta inquieto…Remarkably quiet. The children are upstairs playing some sort of imaginary game that involves a bag of black beans and three Tupperware containers. And miracle of miracles—they are not fighting! The trunks have been packed and await Mauricio's word to transport them next door. The backpacks and kid's little suitcases are stuffed full of their 'essentials'. The only things remaining are the kitchen utensils that we've purchased and I'm considering just leaving them here during the two weeks 'away'. Estamos listo! I think we're ready to go.

The excitement of living in the jungle itself is starting to seep in. The kids are excited about the prospect of sleeping in bunk beds, and I'm excited about the prospect of seeing more wildlife and birds than ever before. There are 500 species of birds that call the rainforest home; we've become familiar with only a dozen or two of them. Sometimes a change of scenery is needed to gain a new perspective on things. And now seems like a good time.

August 8th

And the Rain goes Tap, Tap, Tap . . I think it's safe to say we've entered the rainy season. For five days straight, we've had rain at night, rain during the day, and rain while we go about our daily lives. A never-ending blanket of soft gray extends as far as one can see—beyond the rolling waves, over the mountaintops—everywhere. It's different from the harsh cold gray of winter that I was accustomed to in the northern states. The dark, ominous clumps that used to hang above us for months at a time. Here the gray is more muted. It is spread thinly across the sky to form a barrier between our senses and the sun itself. You can almost feel the sun trying with all it's strength to penetrate through the softness. But to no avail. The rain continues, sometimes with driving force, others with the light tapping that is now a part of our daily stimulus. It blends, like white noise, emanating from the depths of the sky and ending with a caress as it touches the lush green below.

Chapter 22.
The Beginning of the End

August 9th

Last Minute Details... The conversation ended with great relief. On Wednesday, Mauricio and his friend will transport all twelve of our over-fifty-pound-each trunks to the house next door. All have been packed and ready to go, awaiting Colocha's word that now is the time to move things over. I dreaded the day, not knowing how I would possibly manage this daunting task on my own.

Now, we are left only with our overnight bags and a few essentials to be stored at the last minute. I plan to take my laptop computer and camera with me, although the humidity in the midst of the forest is probably not the optimal environment for electronics. Several people I know have constructed 'hot boxes' consisting of a wooden box with a light bulb inside. These boxes are typically open in the front, but provide just enough heat from the bulb to keep corrosion at bay. Perhaps a makeshift box of sorts will serve our needs these next few weeks.

I never realized just how much laundry goes through the perpetual laundry cycle around here. Today I took down everything that has not dried with the past week's rains, along with every towel we own. Yesterday, the sheets and blankets were laundered, picked up just before closing, as we disembarked after the long bus ride from Limon. Quite an expense this is, but really something that cannot be left 'hanging'.

August 10th

Gecko poop on my head... Really, it was the last straw. He was there as I expected, a green gecko, stuck to the wall, sneering at me from high up near the arched ceiling. *Undoubtedly, it was gecko poop that had fallen on my head.*

We've lived with gecko poop now for two months. We step in it when we wake up in the morning, we shake it out of our beds when we lay down at night, and yes, we occasionally catch a falling poop. The clothes hanging on the line nearly always have a white spot or two. Floors are swept a dozen times a day, and still—gecko poop. It's on the countertops, on the stove, on top of the appliances. The fact is, we live with geckos and *sometimes it feels like we live in a zoo.*

August 11th

Birthdays in Paradise... The oriental suite was exquisite. Immaculately decorated and air conditioned, with a burgundy-colored Jacuzzi bath, window seats large enough to sleep on, and last but not least, the master bedroom complete with a lavender silk bedspread. Definitely fit for a princess.

My little nine-year old had all her wishes come true today. I allowed her to play hooky from school, then 'Mama' the local cook from Kaya's Place, baked a chocolate cake with homemade caramel frosting, which we shared with the current inhabitants of Kaya's and some of the BriBri children who were passing on the way home from school. A Jacuzzi bath at the hotel followed, then another bath after dinner. My princess slept in her very own room, on her very own bed, with down pillows, and a thick fluffy comforter, all of silk. Of course, with the air conditioning blowing full blast.

August 12th

T.M.I. or Brain Overload... For all of the excitement of yesterday—the move out of our old house, the party, and the night in Oriental Wonderland, my brain is currently operating on overload.

Our landlord tracked us down at the hotel just as we were ready to ship out this morning—and luckily before we made the final trek into the Jungle. As frequently occurs here, there was a last-minute change of plans. Colocha's daughter and son-in-law were among the unlucky ones to be infested with what is being referred to as the 'plague' of ticks that has recently hit the area. Their house has been overrun, and fumigation is now approaching Day Five. Many have speculated that this latest plague is yet another Biblical sign that the Apocalypse is near.

The reason this affects us is that with the daughter and son-in-law staying down at Playa Negra, we would have been left to fend for ourselves in the jungle, with only the notably untrustworthy front guard to keep us company. It was decided this simply will not do, and a compromise was reached with Mauricio's sister who lives part of the time in the house we were originally supposed to be moved into this week.

So we will be moving next door after all...Part of me was relieved not to have to worry about scorpions and vipers and children in the jungle; the other part was vastly disappointed to miss out on the experience.

I admit—this week has not been a particularly good one. The move caused an upset to everyone's schedules—as much as we stick to a schedule. I allowed the kids to miss the past two days of school. My daughter is now suffering with a terrible head cold, sore throat and fever—probably from the sudden reintroduction to air conditioning. And the rains have stopped, which means the sun is beating down harder than ever.

It's disconcerting to move from place to place to place, sleeping in three beds in as many nights. And it doesn't help to be living on 'the other side of the fence' looking in on the people who now occupy what we've considered 'our' home for the past two months.

The new casita is quite a step up from where we've been living. It's all one level with two bedrooms—although one has been locked up and stores all of the personal items belonging to Mauricio's family. One bunk bed and a single sit pushed up against the walls of the remaining bedroom. The entire house is made of local hardwood, impeccably cut and polished to a glistening sheen. Tung and groove style is used throughout. The shutters in the house all latch from the inside, as those in the other house, but they are much lighter weight and rather than having to struggle with a heavy cross-board, the shutters here have modern sliding metal latches and each one is slatted to allow for air flow. Even with the windows completely secured, it is cool in here this evening.

The noises are different. The view is different. I never realized there is a large yard behind this house where the neighbor's horses graze daily. The distant music we typically hear on the weekends is closer, just beyond the curtain of shrubbery that separates the house from a neighboring cluster of small local Tico structures.

I think the new house will do just fine, once we settle in. Unfortunately, for tonight, every crunch resounds with a thousand echoes throughout the walls. We were used to sleeping upstairs with the windows wide open. Knowing the metal overhang below couldn't possibly hold the weight of a peeping Tom. Luckily, mañana is another day.

August 13th

The grass is always greener... Remember those sleepless nights I mentioned—the ones where the dogs kept a herd of horses at bay all night long?

There is a small brown filly, quite a feisty little thing, which spends the greater portion of the nights neighing incessantly. We saw her in the light of day today, frolicking, dancing on knobby legs. Suddenly, she made a running leap and scaled the barbed wire fence separating the grazing field from the back yard. Of course, this caused a commotion with the kids; they were squealing and running for the camera all at the same time. The horse stopped short a few feet from the fence line, grazing like a half-starved lunatic, and looking up only momentarily to see what tastier treats lay ahead—and to the side—and behind. She was quick to find a rotten pineapple lying on the ground near the back window, and ate the entire thing, leaving only the center core. Some red flowers and a banana tree served as targets number two and three.

Look-a-like mama horse must have missed her baby because not five minutes later, a larger version of the small brown filly came galloping down the side path along the fence line. Baby horse fell in along with mama, except she was still on our side of the bushes. Her run ended abruptly at the corner, near the padlocked gate, where she realized there was no getting out.

Baby horse explored the yard for quite a while, trotting back and forth, swishing her tail at some annoying pest or another. Several times, she ran back to the low double barbed wire she had scaled on the way in, sniffing and snorting anxiously. Finally, mama horse found a way to get to baby, and amidst the frenzied barking of the dogs, they made their way out via the front entrance and galloped on down the road.

Caballos on the Beach

August 15th

Swaying palms... The shade of the palm trees along the beach road stretched just far enough to touch the embankment. The breeze was warm, stronger than usual, and with a hint of salt water in the air. Not yet dusk, but the time of day when the sun begins it's slow decent toward the horizon. The walk from town is always picturesque, differing each time with its little nuances. Today it was the warmth of the breeze that struck me. Some days my eye catches a wispy cloud formation or follows a galloping horse as it runs freely down the beach, with swirls of black sand trailing behind.

Bye, Bye Bicicleta... The first thing my daughter said this morning, on the national holiday for Mother's Day, was, "Mommy, where's your bicycle?" Stolen—along with a pair of tall rubber boots that will invariably be worn by some lucky chapear. While out 'shopping' for a Mother's Day gift, he evidently decided at the last minute to pick up something for himself.

I was not as distressed by the situation as one would think, considering the bicycle is my only mode of transportation. The repercussions of the incident sunk in, however, as I walked back from town later in the afternoon with a heavy bag of laundry slung over my shoulder.

The Denuncia...I approached the open window of the one-room police station and asked to file a 'denuncia' to document the loss of the bicycle. An elderly man in uniform, wearing glasses, but missing his top dentures, motioned for me to come inside and sit. With children perched on chairs peeping over my shoulder, I began the process of 'documentation'. I did this more out of curiosity than the belief that the bicycle will be found. The clerk was friendly enough, though when he poised to ask me a question, he positioned his face no more than a foot from mine and stared directly into my eyes. I had to wonder whether this was some type of ill-taught interrogation technique.

Another elderly man—apparently a friend—sporting a

huge bloodied bandage wrapped around his middle finger, wandered in before my interview was over. The ensuing conversation and the very definite chopping motion he made led me to believe he was just told that the finger would need to be amputated. *Que mala suerte!*

The clerk continued without blinking an eye. He shuffled through a pile of papers looking for what I assumed to be the correct form. In the end, it turned out to be a blank sheet of computer-feed paper, and then another, with a piece of old-fashioned carbon stuck in between. He asked a series of questions, requested my passport number, and hand-wrote the statement in blue ink. My signature was followed by none other than the notoriously huge rubber stamp.

At one point during the interview, the phone rang. Yason! Yason! Phone call for officer Jason. Jason came around to the front window to take the call, wearing pants only. He had been in the process of laundering his shirt out back...

THE DECISION TO RETURN...

The following is an excerpt I wrote several days ago. It will probably come as a surprise to many of you. The words have sat on my computer screen time after time as I pondered the significance of yet another major change in our lives. Now is the time though, to make our plans known, and to begin the progression into yet another season of life.

There are many reasons I moved to Costa Rica and just as many reasons we will return to Florida—less than six months later. The experience has been neither a waste of time nor energy, as I've found a new strength within myself and awakened a renewed sense of creativity that I had long since lost. I've gained a perspective on life that was sorely needed. The sacrifices we made to come here were well worth the investment. I've learned more in three months than I could have possibly learned in the next decade had I stayed where I was, at that point in time in my life. I'm already saddened by the things I will miss about this country, but returning home now does not mean never to see the black sand beaches again. Nothing in this life is permanent; we simply create and change our circumstances to whatever need currently exists.

Sad News... The news of my impending departure traveled quickly and the day was filled with well wishes and teary eyes. I'll never forget the friends I've made here and have already promised myself an annual trip to what has become familiar territory. Since the move to the new house, it seems we are in perpetual 'limbo' with clothing and carry-ons lining the living room wall, and most of our belongings still behind the locked bedroom door. Each day there is another item we realize is not readily available. Last night, it was the potato masher; today it was a flashlight when the power suddenly went out. I plan to discuss our immediate future plans with the landlord tomorrow, and to request the remainder of our things be released from captivity.

August 16th

The final trip to Limon... We took off to Limon today. Partly to escape, but mostly, we went to wander the streets of Limon one last time.

The bus we boarded was not the best; with it's torn seats and dirty windows. By the second stop on the uncharacteristically long trip—over two hours—we were not the only ones to raise an eyebrow every time the brakes were applied. Crunchhhhhh..... Something was definitely off kilter with the mechanics on this particular model. We were fortunate to make it all the way to Limon and, believe it or not, were assigned the very same bus on the return trip. Luck was with us, as we made it home as well.

Caribe Pizza is the typical first stop on our afternoon excursions. Particularly because we are always starved by the time we arrive and arrival time always seems to fall in line with the lunch hour. The restaurant's convenient location just down the block from the bus depot also makes it difficult to succumb to temptation. We ordered the usual—two pequeñas, solo queso, y una pequeña suprema. Add a Coca grande and we're all set. I held the same conversation with the owner as

I've held a dozen times over. All the usual niceties—"How are you, nice day, will you be having the same today?" Then he directs the expected question to the children. "Have you learned any more Spanish since you were here last?" They look at him with blank faces pretending not to understand, but they do. It felt odd to walk out of there today knowing we wouldn't be back—at least not for a very long time. I didn't have the heart to tell him we were leaving.

As we walked toward the concrete wall that lines the water's edge, all three of us suddenly noticed another island, a smaller version of the original, jutting off to the north. We felt sure it was never there before. The second island was not in any of the previous photographs and I was stumped for a while as to how this island had suddenly mutated and become two. It became evident as we traversed a little further, along the concrete wall toward the park, that some sort of optical illusion occurs just as you turn the bend. From the end of the road near the bus depot, the sectioned island looks like it's directly in front of us. Another 200 meters and around the corner in front of Parque Vargas—the island still looks like it's directly in front of us, only this time it is whole again.

The water washes in over the dead coral that was lifted up from the ocean bed during the great quake of '91. It is then rhythmically pulled out again, creating a series of small waterfalls atop each of the coral formations. Such a vast area, stretching a whole City block across and probably twice that in length. I close my eyes and imagine what it must have been like to see the live reefs raising up in their colorful splendor before the sun dried them to light mud-brown.

We sat and watched the island, taking in the people and activity all around. The kids are adept now at ordering from the shaved ice vendors, partly in Spanish, partly in improvised sign language. It's amusing to watch them from a distance. They found a vendor who had some of the coveted 'coco' flavoring and brought back a rainbow of icees—red, orange, and white. I won't get into hygienic reasons, but will only say that these were a vast improvement upon the icees the kids had gotten from the old man in Puerto yesterday.

The trip lasted about six hours from start to finish. We arrived back in Puerto feeling a sense of completion.

Bleu beef? Patagonia is the small restaurant next to the friendly Colombian's gift shop. We've unknowingly passed it by dozens of times. We have in fact even stopped to read the menu—and then walked on. Today, we wandered inside the dirt-floor restaurant and sat down. It turns out to be run by a couple from Argentina—and specializes in something called Argentine Bleu steak. I don't believe another restaurant in town can compete with the tender steak and elegant olive oil and spice dip I was served. The kids ordered chicken breast, also served off the grill, and this was the first meal they've eaten *all of* since we've been here. A lovely tea candle floating in a red liquid accented our table, and the meal ended up being served entirely by candlelight because the power went off in town just as the plates were set down in front of us. *Alex believes God purposely caused the outage so we could enjoy the ambiance of the evening.*

August 18th

4:00 am Expectedly, I have laid awake for most of the night. Our departure is at 10:00 with many details to complete before the van arrives. I sit pondering the next weeks and the tasks that must be accomplished. I am sure that some will view my return as a failure, perhaps as the inability to follow through on my original plans or the lack of gumption to stick with a more intense lifestyle. But within myself, I know the truth—that the past ten weeks have, in fact, been the greatest success of my life. The time that I have spent exploring my own abilities has brought to me a greater peace from within and a better understanding of those closest to me. The friends and contacts I've made here will follow me, I am sure, to the ends of the earth and *nothing is more precious than friendship.*

I leave today not knowing where the tides will carry me.

For now, it is back to Florida where my family is. But I do know there is a whole world out there. Each one of us with our own set of talents, our own unique abilities. It is the sum of the whole that makes the world go round...

5:30 am Daylight now and the birds are out in droves—squawking, tittering, and gliding back and forth as if to bid us safe passage. Already the local men walk down the side path in rubber boots, on their way to work. It is a cool morning with dismal gray clouds; but the telltale specks of sky that promise a warm afternoon are already visible from my vantage point here on the front porch.

The children are still nestled deep within their covers, much like small hibernating animals in the dead of winter. The same covers that need to find a place in our already full luggage. We missed the laundry pick-up last night so another bag of clean clothing will need to somehow be squeezed in prior to leaving town.

The break of the waves resounds strongly in my ears this morning, crashing in a continual pattern along the beachfront. I almost wish we had taken advantage of one last swim yesterday, while we still had the chance. It seems once you live near the sea for awhile the novelty of the water itself loses its luster, leaving in its stead a desire only to rid oneself of the black sand granules that forever cling to the skin.

I can smell the sweet aroma of the plump yellow fruit hanging heavily from the tree across the fence. A tropical delicacy whose name escapes me, this common fruit make a tangy morning drink, albeit with a bit of a kick. The fruit here continually ripens and each morning a half dozen bursting with brilliant color and tangy juice lay on the ground waiting to be gathered up. When we were staying in the other house, an avocado would invariably fall just before dawn, striking the electrical wires, it's bouncy landing pattern coming to a halt just outside the kitchen window.

8:00 am The morning began with walk over to the Stevens to beg a phone call to the airport. I hated to arrive so early, but the e-tickets were sent to me grossly misspelled; and I suspect a correction will need to be made.

The Stevens have a full agenda this morning. Today is a Thursday and will be filled with the typical bustle of people trailing in throughout the day for soup. Since the change in the food bolsa program, the tide seems to have shifted, with more people showing up during the week, and less on Saturday. In the end, the numbers served are the same.

The Health Minister and his staff will be back again today to finalize details of the new free clinic that will be provided to the indigenous people. Daniel took him for a walk up in the foothills yesterday to see the general population that will be served and to get a better idea of existing living conditions.

Constantino, a sweet local indigenous man who peddles bananas and other edibles, will be bringing his elderly mother in this morning to be seen. An exam will be completed somewhere on the porch or inside the house, location and privacy issues forthcoming. Apparently the woman has been ill for quite some time and would prefer to see a local Shaman; however, she has agreed to give conventional medicine a try.

10:00 am Mauricio's chapear staff chose this morning to perform their weekly yard maintenance. The industrial-size weed whackers sent gobs of pollen flying everywhere, including through the slats in the windows, and onto everyone and everything that had once been showered and fresh for the impending trip. The house was hotter than ever, as the new fan had already been given away, and with the pollen came the first allergic reaction I'd had since the move to Costa Rica.

We watched helplessly as the young shuttle driver who had been hired at the last minute got the van stuck backing through the pile of gravel near the entrance gate. Once the vehicle had been freed, it seemed wise to just carry the twelve trunks and six carry on bags through the gate out to the waiting vehicle. The morning to me seemed to be an omen of worse yet to come and I began to dread the four and a half hour ride to San Jose.

We managed to forget the laundry, still waiting to be picked up in town at the Laundromat, and had to do a double-take in front of Jeffrey's before proceeding north. It was nearing the lunch hour by the time we arrived in Limon, so I took the driver's up on their offer to stop for pizza before continuing the journey.

The remainder of the trip was uneventful, rainy as expected through the cloud forest, and clear, as is typical, once we arrived in Alajuela. The driver who had claimed to know the hotel we booked had a little difficulty maneuvering once we neared the busy airport roads, but he did find the place after three phone calls to the hotel staff. Upon arriving, the driver and his buddy unloaded our luggage onto the sidewalk and made a quick getaway.

Lucky for us, an amiable staff member helped the kids and I wrangle the pile of luggage into a ground-floor room. It took up most of the floor space, but we were just glad to have the first leg of the journey behind us.

I spied a few fast-food restaurants on the way into town, and to my dismay, so had the children. I was soon talked into calling a taxi so we could go out for KFC, something we haven't had in months. As it turned out, the KFC was located right down the road, inside of a local shopping mall. Apart from the Spanish-speaking clientele, the mall was identical to any that can be found in the United States. Our evening out in Alejuela was a reminder as to just how secluded we had been in our little Caribbean town for the past few months. The children were somewhat surprised to find that Puerto Viejo was not 'typical' of Costa Rica, an exception rather than the rule.

August 19th

The flight... We awoke at 6:00 am, a full hour before the wake-up knock (no telephone in the room) allowing us to take advantage of the free morning breakfast. Gallo pinto, scrambled eggs with cheese, fresh fruit, fresh bread, juices and coffee made for a substantial meal, and a good start to the long day ahead.

For some reason, the airport valet who took possession of the rolling cart holding our luggage managed to walk us directly to the front of the exceedingly long line and checked us in within ten minutes flat. Perhaps again the result of appearing a bit out of the ordinary.

The flight was overbooked and I was offered a 'deal' for staying one more night—the six extra bags would fly for free, and substantial vouchers for hotel and meal expenses would be provided. It was quite a package, but under the circumstances, I felt unable to accept. We boarded the flight as scheduled at 10:30 am and arrived back in Orlando at 3:30 pm—Florida time.

Here is where the journey ends, and hopefully another will soon begin.

Jungle Mom…Signing Off